MW00619456

A Wizard's Dark Dominion

The Gods and Kings Chronicles

Lee H. Haywood

FREE DOMINION PUBLISHING

Story Consultant and Editor: Kerry Haywood

First Published 2017

Paperback ISBN 978-0-9970810-7-7

www.leehhaywood.com

To my readers.
Let me start at
the beginning.

TABLE OF CONTENTS

I	WIZARDS AND SEERS	1
II	BULLIES AND COWARDS	29
III	FOOLS AND FOLLY	53
IV	PRISONS AND TOMBS	77
V	THE OLD AND THE NEW	96
VI	THE WARDEN AND THE WIZARD	121
VII	MASTER AND APPRENTICE	140
VIII	LETTERS AND SECRETS	156
IX	PLAGUE AND WAR	171
X	FIGHT AND FLIGHT	199
XI	HEROES AND VILLAINS	224
XII	THE MONSTER AND THE NECROMANCER	247
	AFTERWORD	258
	PREVIEW FOR *THE GUARDIAN*	259

A Wizard's Dark Dominion

The Gods and Kings Chronicles

CHAPTER

I

WIZARDS AND SEERS

Death's arrival was imminent.

Cendrik could sense it, a taste on the air that left his mouth feeling sour. He watched as a dozen hunched men crept toward the old abandoned hut, not knowing that their fates were sealed. The men were mere ghostly shadows on the moonless night. The dim glint of the glowing inscriptions on their armor was their only tell. The protective wards were intended to guard the wearer from magical attacks. The armor would not be sufficient, not against the foe they were about to face. Evil resided within that hut, and death awaited any man brave or foolish enough to step over the threshold.

Blessed with the gifts of a seer, Cendrik's intuition was rarely wrong about such matters. People were going to die, it was just a matter of who and how many. He looked around the field.

More men, more grim faces, all crouched low, all doing their best to stay hidden from their adversary. The sour taste in Cendrik's mouth only intensified. Death's shadow shrouded them all.

An involuntary shiver worked its way through Cendrik's body. "The Weaver help me, I'm a coward," he muttered to himself.

"Ain't no one contesting that," said Argan, one of his squadmates. The young soldier sidled up alongside Cendrik, gesturing for him to make room in his hiding spot. Cendrik had taken refuge in a small hollow underneath the trunk of a downed tree. It was enough for one, but cramped for two. Cendrik grunted his discontent as he shifted to accommodate the newcomer.

"It's hard to believe the princess is really in there, eh?" said Argan, as he nestled in amongst the roots and broken branches.

Cendrik shrugged. "Someone's in there. The farmer said two drifters came through town. The man was a Kari who spoke with a funny accent. The farmer never saw the woman's face — she was covered with a veil — but her skin was dark. The farmer's son followed after them. The boy claims he saw them take shelter in the hut for the night. Too many coincidences for it not to be them."

"I don't care what some farmer said. I care what

your third eye foresees." He tapped Cendrik between the eyes. "Ain't that why you're here?"

Cendrik frowned. Whenever people heard that he was a seer, they expected his foresight to be absolute. It was anything but. Sometimes it was just a taste on the tip of his tongue or a twitch in his eyelid. Vague feelings of unease. Fate was rarely forthright with her vision of the future. Instead, the goddess granted him flashing images of what might be.

He let his eyes drift over the host of armed men, catching fragments of each man's future. He saw men lifting unborn children in the air. Others kissing lovers in the night. He saw one man stooped over on a street corner begging with a cup, his legs missing above the knees. Some men had no future at all — they would see the inside of a grave before the next new moon.

When he looked at the hut, his visions grew even more troubling. A cloaked figure reaching toward the heavens. A storm of blades and debris raining down. Amidst the chaos stood Cendrik, grinning maniacally as he stabbed at the air, parrying shadows.

Cendrik decided not to mention such dark tidings to Argan, lest the young soldier think him a madman. "I fear that a lot of men are going to die here tonight," said Cendrik finally.

"Well, ain't that some auspicious news," said Argan. He sucked at his teeth.

"I warned the prince to delay, but he wouldn't listen."

"Would you wait if that demon had your wife?"

The prince was Rudlif Manherm, heir to the Capernican throne. A hot-tempered man in the best of times, Rudlif had been especially mercurial since his wife was taken. Cendrik squinted to the far side of the clearing, catching a glint of polished steel low amongst the ferns. That would be the prince. No doubt he was working himself up into a berserk rage, like a kettle left to boil on an open flame.

Cendrik understood the emotion. He had two younger sisters back home, both teenagers, both targets of young men's desires. He had gotten into his fair share of fights defending their honor over the years. He couldn't imagine what it was like to have your loved one stolen away in the middle of the night by a demon. He found himself balling his fists at the mere thought. Still, rage alone wasn't going to win this battle. He hoped the prince would come to the same conclusion before it was too late.

He turned his attention back to the field. The first wave of attackers had progressed to the midpoint in the clearing. They were being especially cautious. Every step was purposeful. Every footfall silent. No one wanted to sound their approach, not to an adversary as dangerous as this demon. The only slim advantage they had was surprise, and every man knew it.

The old crofter's hut looked innocuous enough. It sat alone and derelict in the middle of the clearing, its exterior decayed by time. Once, someone had farmed this land, a few acres of rocky soil cut straight from the heart of the forest. The gray-blue peaks of the Eng Mountains rose high as a backdrop. Abandoned farms like this were common near the mountains. Following the Sundering, homesteaders headed east in droves, hoping for a new life and fresh opportunities. Most found the realities of frontier life impossible to bear. The mountains marked the beginning of elven territory, and the elves were loathe to suffer men living so close to the border. Raiding parties were common. Villages were burned. Homesteaders were slaughtered. Those with an ounce of wit abandoned all they had and counted themselves lucky.

Nature had done its part retaking the land. The fallow field was already ripe with tall grass and green saplings. A few decades longer and the clearing would vanish altogether. Vines crisscrossed the walls of the hut, resembling black tentacles in the dark of night. The thatched roof was half-collapsed, bare timbers showing. The plank siding hung loose in places. An inky darkness seemed to ooze from the offset panels, spilling out into the surrounding field and strangling everything it touched. That made Cendrik shiver all the more.

The hut was a black box, a place where his intuition could not touch. The events destined to happen within the hut's dark confines were beyond his prediction. There was only one thing that could cloud his intuition in such a manner — the Old Magic. The magic of the Sundered Gods. The magic of the Shadow. Cendrik crossed himself, then decided to cross himself again for good measure.

The attack party was almost to the hut.

Cendrik couldn't keep his legs from shaking. He kept catching glimpses of what was going to happen. A flash of white light. Heat like the sun. Death and blood. A seer's gifts were not for the faint of heart.

"They should turn back," he muttered, his nerves fraying by the second. He had never been more certain something terrible was about to happen in his entire life.

Footsteps sounded in the forest to their rear. Argan drew his sword. Naked steel flashed silver as he stabbed his blade toward the noise.

"Hold," hissed a voice from the gloom.

A host of figures emerged from the depths of the forest, fighting men clad in light armor. At their lead was Sullivan, the king's best tracker. He had a dozen dogs in his hunting pack. They were mean-spirited beasts, the offspring of hounds crossbred with wolves. The pack alpha was the only wolfhound off leash, a mammoth creature that outweighed most men. The rest of the pack was muzzled and chained, each one dragging their handler forward.

Sullivan laughed and pointed to the sky. "The gods favor the hunter on a moonless night."

"Fixing for a fight, Sullivan?" asked Argan, sheathing his blade.

"I'm just the kennel master," said Sullivan, raising his hands in feigned innocence. "I'm here to see to the dogs. I take no part in the fighting." He motioned to his pack. "My hounds, on the other hand..." The handlers were doing all they could to control the beasts and keep them silent.

The alpha crept dangerously close to Cendrik's crotch, teeth bared, slobber dripping. A deep-throated growl issued from his clenched jaws.

Cendrik tried to back away, but he had nowhere to go. The alpha nipped at Cendrik, causing him to flinch like a scared baby. This caused the other men to stifle a laugh.

Gods, I'm a coward.

Sullivan quietly snapped his fingers and hissed. The alpha withdrew, slinking back to Sullivan's side with his ears pinned and tail between his legs. Sullivan nodded toward the attack party. "Ten caps says they don't finish the job."

The attack party had reached the hut. Two men were checking the lock on the front door, while others were seeing if the window shutters were latched. A lone figure clambered up the chimney stack toward the roof. Despite all the motion, Cendrik didn't hear a sound.

"I hope they fail," said Argan.

"Are you eager for death?" pressed Cendrik, glaring angrily. He gestured toward the attack party. "If they fail, you'll be the next through the door."

Argan stroked the pommel of his sword. "I'm eager for glory, friend, I'm eager for riches. The prince promised a hundred silver caps to the man who puts an end to that treacherous bastard's life."

"Good luck with that, lad," said Sullivan. "I'll be letting my hounds collect the prize." The alpha growled at his side.

As far as Cendrik was concerned, both men were crazy. There was no prize to collect on the other side of that door — just death embodied.

Their quarry was Sir Jeremiah, the king's former court magic. A battlemage by training, Sir Jeremiah was considered one of the deadliest men alive. For the better part of two decades he served as the sharpest blade in the king's arsenal. But for reasons unknown to Cendrik, Jeremiah had fallen afoul of the king. He was banished from the land and declared an outlaw. Seeking revenge, Sir Jeremiah broke into the home of Prince Rudlif and stole the princess from her bed. Relying on a mixture of Cendrik's foresight and Sullivan's dogs, they had managed to track him down. They finally had him surrounded.

Funny how it doesn't feel that way, thought Cendrik, as he eyed the hut. In truth, it felt to him the other way around. Cendrik had seen what battlemages were capable of doing, how they moved swifter than the breeze, how they turned the most meager objects into deadly weapons, how even the elements were theirs to control. Battlemages were more akin to gods than men. A swift death awaited anyone who tried to face a battlemage in combat.

That was probably why Cendrik's mouth tasted so sour — death would soon be reaping a bountiful harvest.

The attack party finally made their move. One man jumped down through a hole in the roof, others leapt through the window. The main party broke down the front door and rushed inside. Yelling voices pierced the night. "Stay where you are! Get on the floor. Get on the floor!"

Cendrik gasped in dismay. The soldiers should have killed Sir Jeremiah the moment they laid eyes on him. "What are they doing?" screamed Cendrik.

"There's been a change of orders," said Sullivan. "Prince Rudlif wants Jeremiah alive." He chewed nervously at his lower lip.

Cendrik could only cringe and await the inevitable. If the soldiers had time to speak, Sir Jeremiah had time to react.

A flare of white light cut the darkness. The soldiers' voices turned to screams. A surge of air burst upward from inside the hut, tearing off the remainder of the roof and carrying debris dozens of feet into the air. There were bodies amongst the tangled mess of thatch and lumber. The men came tumbling to the ground, their bodies pinwheeling. The enchanted armor they wore did nothing to break their fall.

There were more screams from inside the hut. Lightning cleaved the air. One stroke. Two strokes.

Three. The bolts landed so close, Cendrik could feel the heat on his face. The thunderous boom rattled his chest, and he feared his heart might stop if they struck any closer. Debris flew everywhere — burning timbers, disembodied limbs, shredded pieces of armor. A helmet came flying through the air and landed at Sullivan's feet. The metal frame was glowing white hot, the leather underlayment was burned to ash.

Cendrik gagged and retched. Death had arrived.

Sullivan cursed under his breath as he turned the helmet over with his foot. His giant wolfhound sniffed hungrily at the burned flesh stuck to the frame. The lust for battle that had been in Argan's eyes earlier in the evening had vanished. Cendrik found he had pissed himself. Thankfully, it was too dark for anyone to tell.

A trumpet blared on the far side of the clearing, a strident blast that rent the night. Prince Rudlif stepped forward, his glistening silver armor making him appear a vengeful specter in the gloom. He pointed his sword toward the hut — this was the signal for the second wave to advance.

A lump entered Cendrik's throat as Fate granted him flashing glimpses of how the battle would unfold.

"You can stay here and cower," said Argan,

struggling to hide the fear in his own voice. "I'm off to collect my fortune." The young soldier crossed himself in the gesture of the faithful, spit in both of his hands, drew his sword, and leapt over the log. He sprinted toward the hut waving his sword overhead like a madman. Throughout the clearing, others did likewise, brave men and fools, all rushing toward their doom.

"You too," barked Sullivan.

"Me?" Cendrik's eyes flared with disbelief.

"You see anyone else?"

Cendrik saw a great many other men, in fact. "I'm no warrior," he managed, his voice coming out in a whine. Cendrik was only here to impress the prince with his strengths as a seer — he never had any intention of actually fighting. He sought an appointment at the Academy Arcanum, and hoped the prince would put in a good word with the Arcane Council if he performed admirably.

"A seer's place is behind the battle line, orchestrating troop movements and plotting counterstrokes," argued Cendrik. "Throwing me into the fray would be a waste of my skills. Besides, I don't even have a blade." Cendrik hoped that would end any debate.

Sullivan slapped a sheathed dagger against Cendrik's chest. "Now you do." He jutted his chin toward the host of men advancing on the hut. "The prince ordered me to send you in, so I'm sending you in. Go! Join the others!"

Cendrik didn't budge, couldn't budge. He was struggling to even breathe. "They're going to die. They're all going to die."

"That's not my concern. Now go, you craven bastard." When Cendrik still didn't move, Sullivan kicked him in the ass. With his heart in his throat, Cendrik crawled over the log. The only thing spurring him into motion was Sullivan's wolfhound nipping at his heels.

The horn blared a second time. Bow strings twanged and a dozen shafts took flight all at once. *Gods, they'll kill the princess,* was Cendrik's first thought. *Gods, they'll kill me, was his second.*

The arrows reached their zenith and hissed down toward the roofless hut, a rain of razorblades. Inexplicably, the empty air above the hut suddenly pulsed with light causing the arrows to change course. The arrows were sent scattering in every perceivable direction. He saw one man take a shaft full in the face. Another man fell to the ground screaming like a dying horse, his stomach pierced through the middle.

A second wave of arrows were loosed. A second pulse of light sent the deadly shafts careening off course. A second set of men fell screaming. The sour taste in Cendrik's mouth was worsening by the second.

Argan, young fool that he was, wasted no time rushing toward the hut. He was the second soldier to reach the door. The man directly before him went rigid the moment he passed over the threshold, the veins in his neck bulging like serpents. Argan shouldered the man aside, raised his sword, then went shooting backward through the air, catapulted by some invisible force. His flailing body tore through the sidewall of the hut, carrying a trail of wooden planks behind him. His body landed with a horrible thud near the edge of the clearing.

Cendrik was horrified. "You have to fight magic with magic," he screamed, but no one was listening. Everyone was mad with bloodlust, and fear, and the thrill of combat.

"He can't kill all of us," yelled an eager soldier, his face black with warpaint.

"For the princess!" roared another. The man took an axe to the hut's rear wall, forging a new path into the interior. With the hut nearly blasted and chopped to ruin, there were half-a-dozen ways to enter. Armed men wearing the livery of the king rushed in from every direction, yelling and cursing, hacking and stabbing. No one seemed to be finding anything other than death once they reached the interior.

Cendrik caught his first glimpse of Sir Jeremiah through the hole created by Argan's body. The battlemage was dressed in a black robe, the fabric flowing in his wake as he spun, his motions as fluid as water. He fended off attackers left and right, sometimes striking with a dagger, other times lashing out with magic. The bodies of men collected at his feet.

Sir Jeremiah's voice rose in challenge. "Stop sending sheep to the slaughter, Prince Rudlif. Come and face me yourself!" The battlemage's face was curled in a grimace as he killed — he seemed to take no joy in the act.

Princess Calycia lay huddled at his feet clutching at a bloody gash in her right thigh. She had somehow been maimed in all the confusion. She wore a dirty traveling cloak, matching trousers, and muddy boots — not exactly the attire of someone stolen from their bed in the middle of the night. In the gloom Cendrik could only vaguely perceive her features — dark skin, curly hair black as jet, lips drawn tight with determination. She clutched a dagger in her free hand. But instead of thrusting the blade into Sir Jeremiah's back, which she had every opportunity to do, she pointed it toward her would-be rescuers.

If Cendrik didn't know better, he would have thought the princess was fighting alongside Sir Jeremiah, not against him. But that didn't make sense. The princess was the victim, Sir Jeremiah the predator. Had Sir Jeremiah somehow managed to poison her mind with his sorcery? Cendrik wasn't given any time to think through the matter. A bearded captain grabbed Cendrik by the scruff of his neck and dragged him forward.

"Into the gap!" roared the captain, as he pulled Cendrik over a field of injured and dying men. With a strong shove, the captain sent Cendrik hurtling headfirst into the hut.

Cendrik's mouth had never tasted so sour in his entire life. He stumbled into the hut, his dagger thrusting forward in his weak hand. Sir Jeremiah turned, flicked his wrist toward Cendrik, and then moved on to face his next foe. For the briefest of moments Cendrik thought the battlemage had simply not seen him. Then, not a second later, something came hissing through the air and embedded itself in the right side of Cendrik's skull.

Cendrik collapsed backward, his body momentarily losing all function. The bearded captain jumped over him, his axe pinwheeling as he tried to hack Sir Jeremiah to pieces. There was more screaming and a bright orange flash, but Cendrik lost sight of the action as his head lolled uselessly toward the ground.

"That man just used me as a shield," sputtered Cendrik in disbelief. "Sir Jeremiah just tried to kill me," managed Cendrik, his disbelief greater still. Drool was cascading from his lower lip and he couldn't get his left hand to move. He pawed at the right side of his head with his functioning hand. He was horrified to discover a finger length of cold iron sticking out of his skull. There was no telling how far it went in.

There's a nail in my head!

He felt his stomach turn over, and he would have pissed himself again had he anything left in his bladder.

The fighting continued, but Cendrik paid it little mind. The fates of other men seemed trivial so long as he had a nail stuck in his skull. He latched his functioning hand around the nailhead and pulled. The nail came loose with an sickening crack. Cendrik's face was suddenly hot and wet as blood came gushing from the wound.

Too much blood. Far too much blood.

He fumbled with the nail, trying to place it back in his skull to clog up the hole. All he managed to do was gouge up the side of his face.

The sour taste in his mouth turned hot as fire.

Aaaah-ooooooooooooh...

The howling of Sullivan's pack rang loud and clear, silencing the cries of fighting and dying men. Cendrik's blood ran cold. The wolfhounds were on the loose.

The dogs came hurtling into the hut. For a brief moment, Cendrik wondered how the dogs would distinguish between friend and foe. They didn't. The alpha wolfhound pounced on the first person he came to, tearing out the man's throat. This sent the rest of the pack into a savage frenzy. If madness was Prince Rudlif's intention, he got more than his heart's desire. Men battled hounds, hounds battled men, and Sir Jeremiah stood amongst it all, battling everybody. There seemed no end to the chaos, until Prince Rudlif stepped into the madness.

"*Re da mujat, retpupri fapato,*" chanted the prince, his frame a mere silhouette standing in the threshold.

Cendrik was aghast, those were the words to a magic spell. He had heard rumors that Prince Rudlif was trained in the arcane arts, but he assumed the stories were just lies. Thunder tolled as lightning split the darkness, striking Sir Jeremiah square in the chest. Sir Jeremiah fell backward, tendrils of smoke emanating from the ghastly wound. The dogs were on him immediately, one on each of his legs, another biting for his throat.

The prince was at his wife's side before Jeremiah hit the ground. "My love, you're injured!"

He tried to help Princess Calycia to her feet, but as he reached for her hand she stabbed with her dagger, the blade aimed for Rudlif's neck. Rudlif caught the blade through his palm, the dagger cutting through his mailed-gauntlet as cleanly as it would have sliced through paper. His eyes flared with genuine surprise.

"Have you gone mad?" he screamed.

The princess did not reply. Instead, she grabbed the handle of the dagger with both her hands and tried to drive the blade into Rudlif's neck, throwing all of her bodyweight behind the effort. Sir Jeremiah had somehow poisoned the princess's mind — Cendrik could come to no other reasonable conclusion.

With the blade jammed through his palm, Rudlif was at a disadvantage. He grabbed the princess's wrist with his free hand, but the princess was impossibly strong. She grunted with exertion, beads of sweet forming on her brow. The blade began to glow, the gemstones set in its fuller flaring brighter and brighter as Rudlif's hand began to bleed. Rudlif was forced to his knees. Slowly but surely the blade crept forward until it was quivering mere inches from his throat.

At the last moment Rudlif lurched sideways, letting the blade plunge into his collarbone instead of his neck. Princess Calycia cried out triumphantly, mistaking the wound for a deathblow. But in the same moment, Rudlif struck with his free hand. His mailed fist smashed into the princess's jaw, twisting her head around so hard Cendrik was surprised it didn't snap her neck. Her body went limp and she fell to the ground, cracking her head against the wall in the process.

"The Shadow curse you," said Rudlif, spitting on his wife's unconscious body. His left palm was pinned to his chest by the glowing dagger. He roared in pain as he pulled the blade free, drawing it first from his shoulder, then from his hand. The blade was glowing white hot, the gemstones pulsing with light as bright as the sun. The blood on the blade popped and boiled. Prince Rudlif threw the dagger aside with disgust. It clanged to a stop beside Cendrik's now useless foot.

"Rudlif!" roared Jeremiah with unbridled rage.

A flare of hot flames illuminated the destroyed hut. The growling cry of the wolfhounds suddenly turned into yelps of terror. The beasts went scampering from the hut, their fur in flames. Sir Jeremiah rose to his feet, his face twisted with a mixture of fury and heartbreak.

"You were supposed to be a weapon for the king," hissed Rudlif, blood gushing from the wound in his shoulder. "A loyal tool to keep the evil at bay. Instead, you're a covetous fool. First you steal the Orb, then you steal my wife. You're a traitor to your own kind."

Jeremiah didn't bother to look at his accuser, he was staring at Calycia's limp body instead. "The Orb was never meant to be handled by mortal hands," said Jeremiah, his voice husky and filled with pain. "As to Calycia, she is a free woman. You'd better pray that she's all right."

"The cur bitch can die for all I care."

A low growl emitted from Sir Jeremiah's throat, bestial and terrifying. An inky shadow crept along the floorboards, collecting around Jeremiah's feet, trailing up his legs and chest and arms. The earth began to shake. The few planks still nailed to the walls rattled loose from their studs. Bodies and blades, armor and lumber began to rise skyward, carried on an unfelt wind that sent them twirling in a maelstrom. "Your doom has arrived," hissed Jeremiah. "Your fate is sealed."

Cendrik watched in breathless horror as the objects in the cyclone spun, every blade, every nail, every plank, every jagged piece of armor, everything turned so that it was aimed dead on Prince Rudlif's body. For once, Cendrik saw fear in the prince's eyes.

Someone has to do something. Someone has to stop this. In a panic, Cendrik looked around the room. He was shocked to discover that there was no one else left alive to intervene.

The vision from earlier suddenly replayed in his head. A cloaked figure reaching toward the heavens, a storm of blades and debris raining down. Amidst the chaos stood Cendrik grinning maniacally as he stabbed at the air, parrying with shadows. Rarely did Fate reveal the future in full. Rarer still was it ever so clear what Cendrik had to do.

Despite his wound and crippling fear, Cendrik lurched into action. He picked up the princess's discarded dagger, the ivory handle already slick with Prince Rudlif's blood, and he stumbled forward on numb legs, his left foot dragging in the dirt. Sir Jeremiah raised his hands toward the heavens, oblivious to Cendrik's approach. An impenetrable wall of debris surrounded them, twirling faster and faster. Sir Jeremiah leveled his finger on Prince

Rudlif, and at the same moment, Cendrik stabbed Sir Jeremiah; once in the small of the back, then again in his right shoulder, and one final time in the side. Cendrik's last stroke left the blade buried to its hilt.

A gasp passed Sir Jeremiah's lips. He looked down, his brow furrowed with surprise. Cendrik gave the traitorous bastard a lopsided grin, then he released the handle of the dagger and fell flat on his face. The roaring wind drew to a sudden halt. Jeremiah's spell was broken. The debris rained down around them, everything crashing back to earth at once.

Sir Jeremiah slumped over, clutching at the handle of the dagger in his side. A slow red trickle trailed down his hip and leg. He managed a few shuffling steps toward the princess's body before his knees gave out.

"The Orb, Jeremiah. Where is it?" Rudlif loomed over Sir Jeremiah's failing body.

Sir Jeremiah didn't respond. His gaze slowly wandered about the ruined hut, until finally his eyes settled on Princess Calycia's face. Hand over hand, he crawled toward the princess.

Rudlif stepped over Jeremiah, blocking his path. "Where did you hide it? Tell me and I will promise you Calycia's safety. If she wants to leave me, that's fine. All you need to do is tell me where's the Orb."

Jeremiah's lips parted, and he mouthed something unintelligible.

Rudlif leaned over, placing his ear close to Jeremiah's lips. "What was that? I couldn't hear you."

"The Orb of Azure is not meant for mortal hands," said Sir Jeremiah. He hacked bloody spit on Rudlif's face.

Rudlif yelled with berserk rage and kicked Sir Jeremiah in the side, again in the groin, and a third time under the chin. The last blow knocked Jeremiah out cold.

Cendrik began to frantically rummage through Jeremiah's clothing, his face showing greater and greater frustration with each pocket he found empty.

"Murrr..."

Cendrik must have made some guttural noise, because Prince Rudlif spun on his heels, his eyes flashing in the dark as he sought the source. His gaze settled on Cendrik.

Rudlif blinked and the frustration vanished from his face. An unctuous smile creased his lips. "Cendrik, the fortuitous seer!" he exclaimed, as he hurried to Cendrik's side. "Bards will sing glory of your heroic act. Wonderful work with the dagger. I really didn't see that one coming, although I bet you did!"

Cendrik was shocked to hear that the prince actually knew his name. Rudlif usually just called him *seer* or *boy*. "I did my best, my lord," said Cendrik. He was surprised to discover his words came out slurred and difficult to comprehend. "I wish I could say my skills did a better job of keeping me unharmed." He pawed at the hole in his head.

Prince Rudlif sucked his teeth as he checked over Cendrik's wound. "That's a nasty one," said the prince, sticking his finger to the hole. His fingers came back flush with blood. "We'll have to see to patching this up." He cut loose a swatch of fabric from a dead man's shirt and began to wrap it around Cendrik's head. The prince chuckled as he worked. "You'll have quite the tale to tell your sisters when you get home."

"You know of my sisters?" managed Cendrik.

"Of course, I make a point of knowing about the things that are important to my men." Rudlif cinched the bandage tight.

Cendrik tried to smile, but his face felt weighted down, his lips and cheeks weren't moving in concert with one another. "You honor me, your Highness."

"No, you do the king an honor by serving the throne with such faith and obedience. The world is full of traitorous scum. Good men are hard to come by. Men with gifts such as yours are rarer still."

"My gifts?"

"It was your intuition that told you when to strike Sir Jeremiah, was it not?"

"I could read his every move," said Cendrik, eager to impress the prince. It was a lie, of course, but he saw no benefit in telling Rudlif the truth — that the only reason he acted was because he had a vision of Sir Jeremiah's death earlier in the evening. "I waited until I knew there was going to be an opening, then I struck."

"Good, very good," said Rudlif, nodding his head with approval. "Do you know how many seers can penetrate the mind of an Old Magic wielder?"

"Very few, I suppose."

"None, save you," said Rudlif. Once again that unctuous smile creased his lips. "I've been waiting a very long time to find someone with your unique set of skills." Rudlif gave Cendrik a hearty slap on the back. "Tell me, do you love your king?"

"More than anything," said Cendrik, knowing what was expected of him.

"Of course you do. And you are willing to spend your life in your king's service, are you not?"

"Yes, your Highness." Cendrik could feel it coming, his appointment to the Academy Arcanum. His dreams were about to come true. The risk had paid off.

Prince Rudlif patted his shoulder. "Sir Jeremiah not only stole my wife. He stole something from the king. Something of great importance and terrible power."

"The Orb of Azure."

Prince Rudlif nodded. "Did your intuition reveal where Sir Jeremiah has the artifact hidden?"

Cendrik wiped drool from his chin. "No, your Highness. But I was focused on the battle. Maybe if I had more time with Sir Jeremiah things might be clearer."

It was another harmless lie — Sir Jeremiah wasn't going to live long enough to prove that Cendrik was a fraud. Sir Jeremiah lay only a few feet away gulping for air. Blood frothed on his lips. He did not have much time left.

The prince grinned. "Time is something I can give you in abundance." Rudlif stuck his fingers between his lips and whistled. A man dressed in the white robe of a healer rushed forward from his hiding spot in the woods.

"I know what you want, Cendrik," continued Prince Rudlif. "Find me the whereabouts of the Orb and I will grant you an appointment to the Academy Arcanum."

"Th-th-thank you, your Highness," stammered Cendrik. He tried to bow, but the motion was lopsided and clumsy. "I will not disappoint you." Or would he? Cendrik wasn't exactly certain what he had just agreed to.

"See that this is true." Prince Rudlif turned his attention back to the healer, who was just then entering the ruined hut. "Make sure Sir Jeremiah doesn't bleed to death," instructed Rudlif. "Our friend Cendrik is only getting started picking apart his mind."

The healer nodded dutifully. Lifting his robe, he carefully stepped over Princess Calycia's unconscious body and took a knee beside Sir Jeremiah. He wordlessly went to work saving the battlemage's life.

As it became apparent Sir Jeremiah was not going to die, Cendrik couldn't help but notice the sour taste returning to his mouth. The lopsided grin slowly faded from his face, and a stark question emerged in his otherwise muddled mind — if the cloaked figure standing in the maelstrom wasn't Sir Jeremiah, whose death had Cendrik foreseen?

CHAPTER

II

BULLIES AND COWARDS

A fine line existed between life and death.

Demetry would know. He had seen death up close more times than he could count. He wrinkled his nose as he rummaged through the undergrowth. There was no mistaking the odor of decay. His subject was not far. Like a hound on a scent, he took in great draughts of air through his nose. *To the east*, he surmised. He pushed on through the underbrush, letting the scent of death guide the way.

Birds chirped overhead in the forest canopy, calling out warning cries as he trudged onward. Every few paces he stopped to sniff and rummage. He was getting closer.

Demetry could gauge how long something had been dead just by the smell. In this instance, the putrid scent of rot had given way to a musty staleness. It spoiled the air with its foulness much like a damp cellar filled with mold. *Three weeks, maybe a month,* Demetry guessed. There wouldn't be much left — just skin and bones.

The foul odor led him to a shallow stream. He parted the fronds of a fern growing along the bank and smiled.

There you are.

The remains of a large doe lay curled around the base of a tree, the body half buried by debris. The unlucky creature must have drowned when the river flooded its banks a few weeks earlier. The carrion birds had long since had their fill. The ants, maggots, and grave worms had come and gone. All that was left were reddish bones and crisp leathery skin covered by thin patches of fur. Demetry was pleased to discover that the skeleton was largely intact. The specimen would suffice.

"Demetry, where are you?" called a voice from further downstream.

"Soon," whispered Demetry to the carcass. He let the brush fall back into place, concealing the body, and waved his hands in the air. "I'm over here!"

"Coming," called a shrill voice in reply. That would be Joshua. The boy came hustling along the stream bank, his short arms and legs pumping as if he was competing in a race. He made for a comical sight, and Demetry was forced to stifle a laugh. Joshua was smaller than any boy his age ought to be — a true runt — and he struggled to traverse the rock-strewn bank. Joshua's face was beet red and his tunic was soaked through with sweat by the time he reached Demetry.

Joshua doubled over, gasping for air. "We need to hide," he managed between forced breaths. "They're right behind me."

"Who?"

"Hanberg and one of those bloody Oswyn twins."

Demetry scowled. Joshua was soft, both physically and emotionally, and it made him the target of just about every bully in the school. "Which Oswyn twin — the big one or the ugly one?"

Joshua made no effort to reply — the stamp of heavy boots signaled the approach of his pursuers. Joshua scampered behind a tree. Demetry shook his head, choosing to stand his ground.

Two boys came hurrying along the bank in fast pursuit. They jumped from rock to rock to avoid getting their feet wet. The foremost boy came forward with effortless strides, a natural athlete with a cocksure confidence to match. Hanberg was his name. He was a year ahead of Demetry in his studies. His lips were upturned in a grin, as if he was the only person privy to some cruel joke. Demetry had little doubt that he and Joshua would soon be on the receiving end of whatever unpleasant thing Hanberg had in mind.

Huffing and puffing to Hanberg's rear was Shep, the muscle of the duo. "Who are you calling ugly?" asked Shep, his face looking especially ugly as he squinted in Demetry's direction.

"Certainly not you, Shep," said Demetry, his voice flat and without a hint of irony. Of the two Oswyn twins, Shep was most definitely the ugly one. Of course, few had the gall to admit it to his face. The large lad was half blind, and had to squint at anything that wasn't directly in front of him. To make matters worse, one too many bouts in the schoolyard had permanently upturned his nose like a pig.

Hanberg waved at the tree Joshua was huddled behind. "We all know you're back there, Joshua. Come on out before I have Shep drag you out."

Joshua slunk from his hiding spot, looking especially ashamed. "I... uh... well, sorry, Demetry. I guess I led them right to you."

Shep feigned a punch in Joshua's direction, causing the small boy to leap back in fright and issue a pitiful yelp. Shep laughed, pleased by Joshua's reaction.

"I knew something was amiss the moment I saw you slinking off from the dormitories," said Hanberg, waving his finger in Joshua's face. "And now I catch you meeting with Demetry. Why am I not surprised? Didn't the headmaster tell you to stay away from him?"

Joshua sullenly kicked at the ground "Yes," he finally muttered.

"And why is that?"

"The headmaster said Demetry has a rotten soul," answered Joshua, purposely avoiding eye contact with Demetry.

"Did you hear that Demetry? The headmaster believes you have a rotten soul." Hanberg was grinning wider than ever.

The four boys lived and went to school in Taper. All who attended the school were touched by the Creator's Blessing in one way or another. Some possessed the gifts of a seer and could predict the outcome to events both great and small, while others were magics, manipulators of the natural world. The majority of the children were the sons of wizards and augurs, men who had won their fame and fortune in the War of Sundering. A small minority were the offspring of great houses, families that possessed the latent strength of the old gods in their bloodlines. Every few generations a magic would be born to otherwise ordinary parents. Such children were shipped off to Taper as soon as they demonstrated the slightest magical traits — a toddler manifesting magic could be as dangerous as a hurricane, or so Demetry had heard.

The rarest variety of pupils attending Taper were boys like Joshua and Demetry, orphans and gutter scum who couldn't identify a single magical forebearer in their family tree. How the gift of magic entered a bloodline so low was beyond anyone's guess.

"What do you two want?" demanded Demetry, crossing his arms and holding his ground.

"My uncle told me to keep an eye on you," said Hanberg. He was Headmaster Rioley's nephew; it was a fact he was always keen on bringing up in a conversation. He began to pace circles around Demetry, drawing dangerously close to the debris pile containing the dead deer. "The headmaster says you're sick in the head. He says you've got maggots in your brain." He jabbed his finger into the side of Demetry's head, grinding his finger back and forth until Demetry was forced to wince away in pain.

"You're just jealous," said Demetry, which was

probably true — most of the older boys were. Demetry was a bit of an anomaly. He arrived to Taper later than most, but he caught up with the other students his age by the end of his first year. By the end of his second year he had surpassed many of the fourth year acolytes in skill. Demetry often overheard the word savant pass the lips of his instructors when they thought he was out of earshot. Demetry attributed his knack for magic to the way his mind worked. He only needed to practice a spell once to have it committed to memory. It made the other boys envious, and it made a certain cohort of them especially mean. Only so many Taper graduates were granted admittance into the Academy Arcanum. Middling students like Hanberg saw Demetry as their competition, a position Demetry by no means relished.

"What sick thing do you think I'm jealous of?" asked Hanberg. "Is it your poverty? Your wretchedness? Your stench?" Hanberg sniffed at the air. "The gods help me. You smell like death. They still haven't been able to wash that stench off you, eh?"

Hanberg was likely smelling the deer, but that was not what he was referencing. Demetry's mother died of the plague when he was young. He spent over a week nestled beside her corpse before he was found by the city magistrate. They had to shave his head and burn his clothes to get the reek off his body. The other boys were not keen on letting the matter rest, no matter how much it hurt Demetry each time they brought it up.

Shep wrinkled his pig nose at Joshua and Demetry. "All you orphans smell like shit."

A simple insult from a simple mind. Demetry tried not to roll his eyes. "Be careful, Shep, you might be smelling yourself."

Shep sniffed at his own armpits. He was one of the dumbest magics Demetry had ever met. The son of a famous battlemage, Shep attended Taper only on the merit of his family name. Demetry doubted Shep had the skill to turn water into ice in the middle of winter. Finding his own stench satisfactory, Shep scowled at Demetry.

"Besides," continued Demetry, "the last I heard, you were halfway to being an orphan yourself."

"My father died in the service of the king," snapped Shep. "That's better than you gutter scum can ever claim."

"Might we all be so lucky," said Joshua, sounding as if he truly meant it.

Demetry raised an eyebrow. "Lucky, is that how Shep's father faired?"

"Watch your mouth, Demetry," growled Shep.

"Fealty to my king and country, until my dying breath," said Demetry, giving the king and his high tower, which stood somewhere far beyond the horizon, a mock salute. "Do you think that's how your father felt in the end, Shep?"

Shep chewed at his lip. His hands slowly curled into fists.

"Nasty creatures, those elves," continued Demetry, knowing full well the perils of goading a bull. "I heard they hacked your old pa up and sent him back to your mother in pieces. She had to pay the undertaker to sew him back together for the funeral. Thing was, there was one piece missing." Demetry stuck his hand between his legs and waggled his little finger at Shep.

Shep lunged forward and grabbed Demetry about the neck. His arm cocked back, his great club fist ready to strike.

"Go ahead, hit me," said Demetry, resisting the impulse to flinch. He could take a punch, he had taken plenty before. "Leave a mark the headmaster can't ignore. We'll see who's cleaning the latrines come dusk."

Hanberg stepped between them and guided Shep's fist back toward the ground. "We don't hit idiots," said Hanberg.

Demetry's shoulders slackened, and he foolishly dropped his guard. He immediately paid for the mistake. Hanberg spun around and kneed Demetry in the groin with so much force Demetry thought he might vomit. Demetry doubled over as a cramping sensation rolled through his body.

Hanberg laughed. "Go ahead, show the headmaster your bruised pride, that is, if you can find it. Feels like I just turned you inside out with my knee."

That it did. Demetry's lower abdomen felt like it was tied in knots. Tears began to well in his eyes. Demetry tried to blink back the tears — he didn't want the other boys to see him cry.

Hanberg gave Demetry's back a sympathetic pat. "There, there, Demetry, have a nice cry." With that mocking gesture, Hanberg left himself exposed. Demetry was tempted to elbow Hanberg in the groin, but decided to call it quits before things spiraled out of control. Head to head, Demetry and Hanberg could probably trade punches all day. But Shep outweighed Demetry by more than a few stones. And Joshua would be about as useful in a fight as a scared mouse, assuming he didn't just turn and run at the first sight of blood. Demetry kept his eyes on the ground and swallowed his pride.

"You disrespected Shep's father. Apologize," demanded Hanberg.

"I'm sorry," squeaked Demetry, his stomach still in knots.

"You're an ass," said Joshua. "When I get back to Taper, I'm heading straight to the headmaster's office."

Shep shoved Joshua into the stream. Joshua fell flat on his rump. The water wasn't more than ankle deep, still, it was enough to drench Joshua from head to toe.

"You'll keep your mouth shut, both of you," said Hanberg, his eyes narrowing. "Or we will have a chat tonight in the dormitory."

Demetry nodded sullenly. Joshua sat shivering in the stream with his mouth hanging agape.

Hanberg and Shep sauntered off, singing merrily as they went. "What happened to the boy who slept on the top bunk of the bed?"

"He fell in the night and cracked his head."

"Oh my, his head?"

"Yes indeed, he's dead!"

The two disappeared around the bend laughing with cruel glee. Joshua watched them go, staring daggers.

"Don't let them see you looking at them like that," said Demetry. He pulled Joshua onto dry ground. "I'm sure they'd be happy for a second round."

Joshua spit. "On the street, hollow tongued fools like Hanberg would get knifed in their sleep." He shook his head with frustration.

"And boys like Shep?"

"They'd be the ones doing the knifing." Joshua dropped his chin and stared at the ground. "I should have just hit him," muttered Joshua, balling his little fists. He looked like he might cry.

"Aye? That would have been all of the excuse Shep needed to beat you bloody." Demetry felt awful. Joshua had spoken up in his defense, and what was the boy's reward — a cold bath and bruised pride. He ruffled Joshua's hair. "What do I always tell you?"

"We beat 'em with our knowledge. We beat 'em with our skill." Joshua rapped his knuckles against his head. "We outcasts stick together, right?"

"That's right," said Demetry. He straightened Joshua's tunic, which was pulled askew from his fall. "Why are you still wearing these rags, anyway?" The season had long since turned to fall, yet Joshua still wore the same threadbare clothing he had lived in all summer. His trousers fell short of his ankles and his sweat-stained shirt looked ready to split at the seams.

"It's what I've got," said Joshua, his voice edged with a degree of shame.

Demetry understood the feeling all too well. While the young lordlings like Shep and Hanberg received regular care packages from their parents, those who were wards of the school were lucky if they received a new set of clothes at the turn of each season. Every ward was paired with a patron, most of whom were instructors at the school. Demetry's patron was an elderly magic with a middle-aged son. Demetry's clothes were all hand-me-downs, but he never wanted for attire appropriate for the season. In fact, he sometimes even dressed better than the rich lads.

Joshua was not so lucky. Joshua's patron was Headmaster Rioley. The headmaster had never shown Joshua an ounce of affection. Joshua was an afterthought, a nuisance, good for chores but not much else. Demetry could almost understand why Joshua was treated so poorly, because Joshua, was, well, Joshua.

The boy looked especially pitiful right now in his undersized clothes, drenched from head to toe. He reminded Demetry of an owl caught out in a downpour. "I have an extra cloak back in the dorm," said Demetry. "It will be a little large, but at the rate you're growing it will be a proper fit soon enough."

"Thanks," muttered Joshua, kicking at a stone and avoiding eye contact. None of the orphan boys were especially adept at showing gratitude.

Demetry put his arm around Joshua and guided him away from the stream. "You're all soaked through. How about we head back to the dorms?"

Joshua stiffened his lip and shrugged off Demetry's arm. "No. We came out here to practice, so let's practice."

Demetry was not surprised by the answer. Joshua had spent the better part of his young life on the streets, his magical gifts exploited by a gang of criminals. Untrained, and without a mentor, his ability to use magic was based purely on instinct. This proved a most dangerous combination. One fateful afternoon he lost control of his powers and accidentally burned down an entire bazaar. The Arcane Council picked him up following the incident and brought him to Taper. He was put under the guardianship of Headmaster Rioley to prevent such a catastrophic accident from happening again.

Thankfully, his outbursts were now under control. But having started his schooling so late, his powers currently outmatched his training. He had the strength to perform spells typically reserved for a fourth year acolyte, but controlling his manifestations was a different story entirely. Joshua tried to overcome this deficiency by practicing as often as possible.

"What spell did you have in mind?" asked Joshua, genuinely eager. "We've been studying levitation in my class." He muttered a few words in the old tongue and waved his hands. Dozens of river rocks suddenly rose from the stream, the fist-sized rocks floating on nothing but the breeze. Joshua pinwheeled his arms, and one by one, the river rocks began to collect in stacked cairns along the shoreline.

"Manipulation of the inanimate, yes, but this was not exactly what I had in mind." Demetry produced a red leather-bound book from his satchel, its pages torn and singed.

Joshua's eyes went wide. He crossed himself and took a step back. "Blessed Guardian, where did you get that?" He frantically searched the forest with his eyes to make sure they were alone. "The *Paserani Haote* is forbidden. It should have been destroyed," he whispered.

Demetry showed Joshua the burn marks that wreathed the binding. "It looks like someone tried to dispose of it, then had a change of heart. I found it buried under some other books while I was cleaning the headmaster's study."

"You've read it?" Then with a nod, "Of course you've read it." Joshua scowled, his face twisted with a mixture of intrigue and concern. "That's Shadow worshiper doctrine, Demetry."

"Undeniable," said Demetry with a dismissive shrug. Within the great pantheon of gods, full of saints and devils, deities and demigods, there was one overarching theme — extol the Guardians, shun the Wyrm, and damn all things associated with the Shadow. Demetry found such narrow-minded views of good and evil to be too limiting.

"There's knowledge in here that our elders wish to deny us," said Demetry, clutching the book to his chest as if it were his most prized possession. "Spells and incantations that the Arcane Council seeks to have stricken from the records. As far as I'm concerned, the destruction of knowledge is the greatest sin of all."

"Lies aren't knowledge." Joshua jutted out his lower lip in a gesture that was meant to look stern, but instead ended up looking like a pout.

"These aren't lies, Joshua. They're hidden truths. Secrets the gods wished us never to know. Have a look for yourself." Demetry offered Joshua the book.

Joshua raised his hands and backed away. "I'm

not touching it."

"I said I would train you, teach you things the other boys don't know, give you an edge, so the next time Hanberg and his thug friends come along you might be able to defend yourself. You want to be more skilled than the other boys? You need to practice the things the others boys are afraid to try."

Joshua's shoulders slackened, his eyes slowly wandered back to the book in Demetry's hand. Demetry grinned. Joshua's resolve was breaking down. The temptation was too great. Joshua issued a heavy sigh, a vain attempt to feign displeasure, and snatched the book out of Demetry's hands. "I'll have a look." Joshua plopped down on top of a rock and spread the book open on his knees. His face flickered with a mixture of fascination and horror as he discovered the contents of the forbidden text.

Demetry peered over Joshua's shoulder, noting the pages he stopped on, noting the pages he quickly turned. Demetry couldn't help but smile. He had half-expected Joshua to balk at the mere mention of the *Paserani Haote*. There had once been thousands of copies of the book in circulation, but almost all had been destroyed. Shadow worship was forbidden. Anyone caught in possession of the book was subject to the king's justice.

Joshua sounded off the headings of various chapters as he thumbed through the pages. "The Perversion of Calaban. On the Fallacy of the Guardian's Doctrine. The Splintering of the One Soul and its Implications." He shook his head. "The gods help me. There's enough foul teachings within this text to condemn a soul for all eternity. It's sacrilege, every word of it. I can see why the Arcane Council ordered the book destroyed."

"Paseran was no saint."

"One thing we can agree on."

"But he was a god."

Joshua did not object, although the claim was strongly denied by their teachers. Paseran, Valio, the Shadow — they were all names for the same dark deity. In an age long past, the gods waged war against Paseran. Empires were destroyed and entire continents were closed to the living. Or so the legends told. Now, Paseran was little more than a myth, a scary tale to frighten children at night. But as with all myths, some elements of the tale were rooted in fact, of this Demetry was sure.

"Some say Paseran is the source of all magic within the race of man," continued Demetry. "If this is true, the pages of this book are not filled with heretical teachings — it is a letter from a grandsire to his offspring."

Joshua raised his brow cynically.

Demetry waved off the boy's doubt and reached over his shoulder, turning the page to a dog-eared section near the back of the book. *Epicaj'cacanit,* read the heading on the page. It was the script of a long dead people from a long dead land, but Demetry knew the translation all too well. *Necromancy.*

"Sacrilege," muttered Joshua, his eyes already reading the words to the spell.

"Sacrilege, heresy, sin. Simple words said by simple men who refuse to challenge the established order." Demetry walked toward the riverbank, waving for Joshua to follow. "This way. Our subject awaits."

"Our subject?" Joshua's voice sounded with hesitation, but his actions showed willingness. He hastily scampered after Demetry.

Demetry parted the brush, revealing the carcass of the deer.

Joshua recoiled, raising the cuff of his sleeve to his nose. "A deer? I don't know."

Demetry knelt beside the deer, pulling away the limbs and debris that had collected on the poor creature's body. "I've been turning rats since before we met. I turned old Sullivan's dog after it was gored to death by a boar. How can a deer be any different?"

"It likely won't be, it just feels, well, wrong. You know what the headmaster has to say about Shadow magic."

Demetry knew the headmaster's opinion all too well. He only needed to hear the lecture once to know it would be unwise to be caught dabbling in the dark arts ever again. That's why he practiced in secret, out here in the forest, far from the watchful eyes of his narrow-minded instructors. Demetry shrugged dismissively. "If we were not intended to use necromancy, why did the gods endow us with the gift?"

"To tempt us."

"Do you really believe that?"

"It's what I heard the headmaster say." Joshua starred down down at his own feet.

Demetry snorted. "The old bastard spouts a lot of opinions about a lot of things. If he is so opposed to Shadow magic, why does he own a copy of the book?"

Joshua stared at the deer. "Will it hurt? I mean will it hurt the deer?"

"Dead is dead," said Demetry, mostly believing it. "The soul has long since flown. You will be animating the inanimate, nothing more. It's like floating rocks." Demetry pointed to the still parted page of the book. "You can do this."

Joshua nodded and carefully read over the spell. "Yes, I believe I can. But should I?"

"Only you can make that decision." Demetry settled back against a tree and spread his arms, palms outward, dismissing himself from the choice.

Joshua's hands were trembling as he knelt alongside the deer and laid the book on the ground. He squinted at the text, reading over a few lines at a time and then practicing the directions. He hovered his hands over the bony frame of the animal, swinging his arms this way and that until he got the motions just right. At its root, magic was all about closing out distraction and focusing one's mind on the task at hand. The hand motions and words were just a way for Joshua to focus. It was not so different from a monk chanting a mantra during meditation.

"Just like floating rocks," muttered Joshua, trying to draw confidence from the idea. He made several false starts, uttering the first word of the passage, only to stop suddenly and review the text. Finally, after many careful reads, he began.

"*Cotist rit osasrio re epicaj, tocasis rit rapuss...*," sang Joshua, his voice rising and falling to a melody no one else could hear.

Demetry closed his eyes and mouthed the words himself. The ancient tongue was a lovely language and possessed an ebb and flow that the common tongue simply lacked. Demetry was lulled into an almost dream-like state, the words conjuring up images in his head — of life, of death, of rebirth. It was a never-ending cycle, played over and over again for countless ages. All adhered to this endless dance. The stars in the heavens. The trees in the forest. The mortal races that now encompassed the world like ants.

But suddenly, a jarring word fell into the rhythm that Demetry knew was out of place. The vision tumbled away. The stars swirled to black nothingness, the trees turned to ash. The world of men was crushed by oozing black tentacles, and everywhere he looked a dark shadow encroached. Demetry forced his eyes open.

"*Osario isifi umusat...,*" continued Joshua, oblivious to his mistake.

Demetry's eyes narrowed. Had Joshua misspoken, or was Demetry simply imagining things? A sharp crackle sounded, confirming Demetry's worst fear — the spell was failing. The verse had driven Joshua into a trance. Unaware of what was happening, he continued on with the spell. The crackle became a torrent. The forest began to shiver, the limbs and branches vibrating so fast they began to splinter apart. The soil beneath Demetry's feet began to shift like quick sand. The water in the nearby stream reversed course. Demetry tried to open his mouth and yell out a warning, but his tongue clacked useless in his bone-dry mouth.

The spell came undone with terrifying effect, lighting up the clearing in a ball of white flame. It started beneath Joshua's outstretched hands then streaked outward with horrific force, catching Joshua's body and sending ripples of energy surging through his frame. His body whipped and twisted like a noodle in boiling water.

Demetry dove to the ground and threw his arms over his face just in time. The tree nearest Joshua splintered apart at the base, its trunk reduced to kindling. The wind howled, followed by a biting cold that caused Demetry's breath to catch in his throat. Demetry felt a pain in his scalp, as sharp as a devil ant's sting, then another in his buttocks and thigh. Thumbnail-sized stones became deadly projectiles, particles of dirt hissed by with enough speed to shred clothing.

"The Guardians protect me," cried Demetry, praying that he might survive the chaos. Unfortunately for him, necromancy was the providence of Paseran. And as the forest began to fall apart all around him, Demetry realized he was praying to the wrong god.

CHAPTER
III

FOOLS AND FOLLY

The chaos stopped as quickly as it began. The biting chill faded to warmth. The roaring wind calmed to a gentle breeze. Stones that a moment earlier had been whizzing through the air, thudded harmlessly back to earth. Limbs clattered to a rest amongst the underbrush. Only the soft clack of singed leaves drifting lazily to the ground broke the silence.

Demetry cautiously lifted his head. A shroud of dust hung over the land. All was obscured in shadow, indistinct shapes, shades of gray accompanied by deep blacks. Rays of diffused light cut through the haze. It took Demetry a moment to locate Joshua; his body lay oddly contorted, pressed around the trunk of a tree as if he were giving it a hug. He was motionless, his head flat against the bark, his red mouth agape, his eyes fixed upon the heavens.

"Joshua?" managed Demetry, his voice cracking with fear.

The blast from the backfiring spell was forceful enough to knock a man unconscious. Perhaps Joshua would wake up in a moment and be just fine.

Demetry scurried on all fours over to Joshua's side and pried his friend's body away from the tree. Joshua's head rolled limply as Demetry took the boy's weight in his arms. Panic seized Demetry like a noose. He tried to clean the debris from Joshua's cheeks and forehead, but all he managed to do was smear the blood. Demetry searched for the telltale rise and fall of Joshua's chest, the dull thud of a pulse in his neck, any indication of life at all. He found none.

"It doesn't happen like this, it just doesn't," said Demetry breathlessly. He gently shook Joshua's body, as if trying to awaken the boy from a deep slumber. But Demetry knew better. Joshua was in the deepest slumber of all.

Dreamless.

Thoughtless.

Dead.

Demetry moaned woefully, his cry sounding like the bray of a stricken animal, and collapsed atop

Joshua's body. How long he lay there with hot tears rolling down his cheeks, Demetry could not say. A heartbeat, a minute, an hour. The sun shifted across the sky. The shadows of the forest crept longer and longer until Demetry found himself lying completely in shadow.

How could this have happened? Joshua was just a boy, a child, really. His life had been cruel from the start, living on the street, begging to survive. How could a boy so pure and innocent deserve such an unlucky fate? He didn't, he couldn't. A just god would have never allowed this to happen. The Guardians, the Weaver, Fate — Demetry cursed them each in turn.

Then another thought entered Demetry's head — a realization that chilled him to the bone.

"The gods didn't do this. I did."

Demetry scurried away from Joshua's body, as if distance might absolve him of his sin. Was he responsible for what just happened? Was he to blame? Demetry's mind raced feverishly. The world was spinning around him, the shadows creeping, creeping.

He cried out in prayer. "Blessed Ones, help me in my time of need." His words were hardly a whisper, and they brought him no comfort. He had discovered the book. He had taken it from

Headmaster Rioley's study. He was the one who goaded Joshua into attempting the spell. There would be no forgiveness. Demetry would pay for this crime in blood.

"Blessed Guardians," he gasped in terror.

Demetry eyed the book. The cover of the Paserani Haote was pockmarked from the explosion, but the pages themselves were still intact. If he acted quickly, he could return the book to the headmaster's study; Headmaster Rioley might not even notice it was touched. Then he could lie about what Joshua was doing. He could...

Demetry pulled the book closer, reopening it to the dogeared page.

Headmaster Rioley had a favorite quote. *"Fear causes weak men to cower, wise men to take action, and foolish men to perform incomprehensible acts."*

What Demetry now pondered was incomprehensible, yes, but there was wisdom there as well, a deep cunning, a path forward that might save Demetry and Joshua both.

He examined the text carefully, reading it slowly, word by word, studying it closer than he had ever done before. He considered the meaning of each word, translating the ancient script in his head. He focused on the rhythmic patterns, noting the words that rhymed and the words that did not.

There was a type of necromancy Demetry had failed to mention to Joshua — soul binding. It tied the soul of the deceased person to their body. The spell had to be performed soon after death, before the soul was able to vacate the body. But if done properly, the body and soul would be bound for all eternity. Sentience would be restored, the flesh would regrow, old wounds would heal. Joshua would rejoin the world of the living. Outwardly, he would appear as he did before. But, as Demetry knew all too well, Joshua would never be the same. A shadow of the afterlife would haunt him forever. Neither dead, nor alive, he would be a being who straddled both worlds, a wraith.

Demetry had performed the spell once before. His subject — a rat. The soul bound rat was different from any other creature Demetry had raised from the dead. The rat would flee when startled and eat when presented food, yet when Demetry held the rat underwater it would not put up the slightest resistance. Something was missing, a key instinct — a will to survive. But that was just a rat. Certainly it would be different with a person. Certainly it would be different with Joshua.

Demetry surveyed the forest. The dust had long since settled. The sun was sitting low on the horizon, painting the treetops with crimson light.

The ceaseless babble of the nearby stream was accompanied by the chirp of songbirds. All was green and peaceful. Harmony was restored. Only Joshua looked out of place, his frail body twisted in death.

"You deserve better," whispered Demetry into Joshua's unhearing ear. "If I cannot grant you life, I will give you the next best thing."

Demetry sat upright, steadfast with resolve. This was what had to be done, there was simply no other option. Demetry closed his eyes and began to chant. "*Cotist rit osasrio re epicaj, tocasis rit rapuss.*" His voice rose and fell with the rhythm of the spell. He pronounced each word with practiced precision, yet in his head, he heard only the same word spoken again and again.

Rise.

Rise.

Rise!

A slow, wretched, gurgle emitted from Joshua's throat.

Demetry leapt back in fright, his reflexes getting the better of him. He knew it wouldn't be pretty — the resurrection of the dead never was. Still, he had never gotten used to seeing the dead return to the world of the living.

Joshua began to violently spasm. His muscles

convulsed. His back arched and jerked. A low moan welled from deep within Joshua's chest and a surge of blood came flowing from his gaping mouth, spilling down his cheeks and filling his nostrils. His hands clawed at the earth, digging deep furrows. His legs thudded against the damp soil. Demetry reached for Joshua's ankle, hoping to halt the boy's seizing frame. Joshua kicked him squarely in the nose, causing Demetry's vision to blur in a strobe of light. Then, as quickly as it began, Joshua settled back to the ground and lay motionless.

Demetry rubbed at his aching nose, his eyes welling with unwelcome tears. He ignored the pain, focusing on what really mattered. "Joshua, are you all right? Please, speak to me, take my hand, anything. Show me that you're okay."

Ever so slowly Joshua complied, lurching to his knees, then his feet. A trickle of blood steadily dripped from his lower lip, running down his chin and staining his shirt red. His pupils were black pools that spanned from lid to lid. His cold dead eyes did not stray from Demetry's face.

Demetry attempted to speak, but his voice merely quivered. Whatever hope remained was demented and without reason. "We have to clean you up," he finally managed.

Demetry timidly reached toward Joshua's deformed figure, but at the last instant he recoiled, fearful to touch the pale skin. "We can't let the headmaster find out about this. He can never know. This will be our secret, right? I will be sent away if they find out what happened here. They..." His voice trailed off. They were not alone.

"The gods help me, what have you two dullards done?"

A cold shiver ran down Demetry's spine. Shep and Hanberg were standing at the edge of the clearing. Shep was squinting at the scene. Hanberg was grinning from ear to ear.

"Damn near burned down the forest," said Shep, picking up a blackened leaf. It crumbled to ash in his hand.

"Tsk, tsk, tsk." Hanberg brushed his fingers together like a chiding mother. "Gone and bloodied yourself, I see. You're not supposed to practice spells off of school grounds. What will the headmaster have to say about this?"

"Nothing," said Demetry, his voice sounding much braver than he actually felt. "Because you're not going to say a word. As I remember, you're the one who bloodied Joshua's face. Isn't that right, Joshua?"

Joshua made no effort to reply. Or nod, or

blink, or breathe. He stood beside Demetry, swaying silently to some unfelt breeze. Neither of the boys seemed to comprehend the true nature of Joshua's condition — for now they were both focused on Demetry.

"All I did was shove him in the water," said Shep, raising his hands, palms outward. "I didn't do that to his face."

"That's not how I remember it," snapped Demetry.

Hanberg smirked. "Feeling clever, huh? You're not as clever as you think." His eyes wandered to the forest floor. Demetry's heart stopped. *The Paserani Haote.* The book was lying on the ground, opened to the spell for necromancy. Hanberg was still too far away to read what was written on the page, but that would not last.

Demetry leaned over and collected the book, trying his best to appear nonchalant. He quickly returned the book to his satchel. "So what? I borrowed a spell book from the headmaster's library. You'd be lying if you said you haven't done the exact same thing."

"Yeah? Well I've never gotten caught," said Hanberg with a laugh. He pointed at Demetry's satchel. "Shep, fetch me the book. Let's see what these fools were practicing."

Shep was on Demetry before he could resist, locking his big burly arm around Demetry's neck. He twisted Demetry's wrist painfully, forcing him to release the satchel from his grasp. Shep tossed the bag to Hanberg.

Hanberg upturned the satchel into his hand, pouring out the contents. It only took him half a heartbeat to read the book's title. He tossed the book aside in disgust, his face contorting as if he had just handled a poisonous snake. "The gods help me!"

"What is it?" asked Shep, his arms still locked around Demetry's neck.

Hanberg's eyes wandered to Joshua with newfound understanding. For once, he looked genuinely horrified. "Sinner. Dark wielder. Shadow worshiper," he hissed, spitting out each title with greater and greater disgust. He leveled his finger on Demetry. "Necromancer!"

Shep threw Demetry to the ground and proceeded to wipe his hands clean on his trousers, as if he was some how tainted by coming into contact with Demetry's flesh.

"You're damned, Demetry," said Hanberg, regaining a degree of composure. "They hang men for the crime of necromancy." He drew a line in the dirt with his foot. "Shep, make sure Demetry, and this... this thing, don't go anywhere. I'm going to fetch the school elders. They'll know what to do." Hanberg darted off into the woods.

Widening his stance, Shep placed a balled fists on either of his hips, doing his best imitation of a soldier on guard detail. He gave a low whistle. "You're in for it now, Demetry." said Shep. He seemed eager for a conversation, anything to distract from Joshua's wretched state. "You'll be lucky if you get the noose. The Arcane Council will likely want to make an example of you." He ran his finger along his gut as if it were a knife.

"I didn't do this to him," said Demetry, half meaning it. He waved a finger at Joshua. "Joshua was practicing a spell. He misspoke. It backfired. Tell him Joshua. Say something."

Joshua remained silent, still swaying, still staring at the same spot on the forest floor. A trickle of red spittle dripped from his lower lip. *Drip. Drip. Drip.*

Why wasn't Joshua chiming in? Had the spell failed? Had Joshua's soul already flown? Had Demetry risked all only to raise an empty husk? He struggled to keep the frustration from showing on his face.

Run away. Disappear into the woods. Head north.

Yes, that was a reasonable idea. The elves were always looking for turncoat magics. Demetry wasn't the most skilled, but maybe they would look past that fact.

"Shep, what if you just let me walk away," said Demetry, knowing full well that he would have better luck pleading with an ogre. "By the time the school elders arrive I'll be long gone."

Shep sucked his teeth and spit. "It won't be no use. The dogs will find you. It won't even be a contest. Old Sullivan's hounds will sniff you out quick as that." He snapped his fingers to emphasize his point. "If I were you, I'd just kill myself. Go jump in the stream and swallow some water. You'd be doing all of us a favor." Shep grinned devilishly. He seemed genuinely hopeful that Demetry would follow his instruction.

"You're a pig, Shep," snapped Demetry, his desperation shifting to rage.

"Aye, well you're a useless waif. My mum always wondered why they let homeless bastards like you into the school. They're dangerous, she always said. Too many years without structure. Too many years using the Old Magic." He tapped his skull. "It perverts the mind, brings you too close to the Shadow." Shep's eyes darted to Joshua. "Hey, what's he doing?"

Joshua had inexplicably begun to move, heading off at a leisurely pace into forest.

"Joshua, get back here," commanded Shep.

Joshua didn't reply. Of course he didn't reply. Shep was too obtuse to comprehend the nature of Joshua's current state. Although in truth, Demetry didn't understand it all that well either.

Clearly flustered, Shep's eyes darted from Demetry to Joshua and back again. He didn't seem to know what to do. "Make him stop!"

Demetry threw up his hands. "I have no control over him." Or did he? The only thing Demetry knew for certain was that Headmaster Rioley and the other school elders could not know what happened.

Suddenly, Joshua broke into a galloping sprint. It was as if all of his joints were out of alignment. His gait was almost bestial in nature. His speed would be difficult to match.

Shep watched him go, slack-jawed.

Now is your chance. Flee.

For some reason Demetry didn't budge. Perhaps it was fascination, perhaps it was fear. Whichever it was, Demetry felt oddly enthralled. There was an ugliness about Joshua's loping gait, but there was a strength there as well. The Joshua he knew was gone, leaving behind a voided body that was strong, inexhaustible, and unflinching; a tool that could be as deftly utilized as the sharpest sword or the hardest hammer, that is, if the puppeteer knew the right commands.

For the briefest of moments Demetry envisioned a world overrun by the dead, but it was not a nightmare. Automatons laboring in the field, building roads, manning the battlements, their actions ceaseless and relentless, all turned toward the greater good. Empires would fall. Slavery and serfdom would cease to exist. Each man would be free to endeavor in whatever pursuit he so desired. It would be a new beginning for all men, rich and poor, highborn or low. A few talented magics might accomplish what the Sundered Gods had failed to achieve — paradise.

Demetry blinked and the vision turned to ash, leaving nothing but a stale taste in his mouth. A voice that was not quite his own was screaming in his head. *"Go, run while Shep is distracted!"*

Shep took a step toward Joshua, unsure what to do. Demetry seized the opening and leapt on Shep's back. He locked his forearm around Shep's neck, and held on, straining to pull Shep to the ground. It was like trying to tackle a bull. One second he was on Shep's back, the next, he was flying through the air. Demetry landed face first on the ground, and before he could regain his feet, Shep kicked him in the side, knocking the wind from his lungs. Demetry rolled back and forth struggling to catch his breath.

"The gods help me, what do I do?" muttered Shep, his eyes darting between Demetry and Joshua. He threw his hands up in despair and ran after Joshua, screaming, "Get back here!" Joshua was now so far away he had fallen from view.

"Flee! Flee! Flee!" screamed the voice in Demetry's head.

Demetry was alone, momentarily free to forge his own future. If he forded the stream and headed north he could reach the Luthuanian border in under a week. The journey would be perilous, but hope of salvation lay at the end. The elves would give him asylum. Surely they would.

"Or they'll cut you into pieces, just like they did Shep's father."

He shook his head, knowing he must not think like that. *A coward is paralyzed by fear*, he reminded himself. Now was his chance, his only opportunity to turn aside from his sin.

Demetry walked to the edge of the stream. The water was shallow, no more than knee deep in the middle. All he had to do was take one step forward, and then another, yet something was holding him back. Taper was his home, all he had. He remembered what it was like to have nothing. No family, no friends, no place to lay his head at night.

Never again.

There was still a way to fix this, Demetry was certain. Cruel boys do cruel things, and Hanberg and Shep were the cruelest of them all. Everyone knew it, even the school elders. Demetry would only have to tell a few simple lies to turn the accusative finger the other way around. Shep and Hanberg chased Joshua out of town — surely someone saw it. Then things got out of hand. They hit Demetry — he had the bruises to prove it — and accidentally killed Joshua. Hanberg tried to cover his tracks by raising Joshua from the dead.

This could work, thought Demetry. The best lies were the ones based on truth, after all.

Demetry rushed to pick up the book from where Hanberg had thrown it and chased after Shep and Joshua.

"*The plan might work*," agreed the voice in his head. "*But you can't let the other boys reach the headmaster first.*"

Demetry doubled his pace, plowing through the forest at a break-neck speed, completely careless of pitfalls and debris. Not far ahead he head a scream. Shep had caught up with Joshua.

Demetry suddenly tasted blood, his throat becoming rich with the hint of hot iron. He spit, certain he must have bitten his tongue. His saliva came out clear. "Not good, not good at all," muttered Demetry.

Upon cresting the next hill, he was greeted by a low pitiful moan. Shep lay at the bottom of the valley, his back pressed against a tree, his left leg bending where there wasn't a joint. Demetry thought he saw bone... and teeth marks.

"He b-b-bit me," stammered Shep. A hunk of flesh was missing from his forearm. The wound was gushing blood. His face was as pale as ivory. Beads of sweet glistened on his brow. Shep had removed his belt, and it rested in his trembling hand. He clearly intended to use it as a tourniquet, but he seemed unable to cinch it tight enough to stem the flow of blood. He held the belt out to Demetry, a wordless cry for help. For once in his life Demetry saw that pleading look in someone else's eyes. It gave him an odd pleasure.

"Let the bastard bleed," said a voice only Demetry could hear.

Demetry took the belt from Shep's trembling hand and threw it out of reach. Shep was beyond words. He simply lowered his chin to his chest and closed his eyes in resignation.

Demetry pressed on, sprinting as fast as his legs could take him. He cleared the forest, entering the communal farmland that wreathed the village of Taper. Demetry ran straight across the field, not bothering to take the road that bisected the land. Joshua and Hanberg had obviously traversed this same route and made a scene. A half-dozen laborers were gathered in the field to tend to the harvest, yet no one was working. They were all standing upright, squinting off into the distance in the direction of Taper.

Upon entering the outskirts of town, Demetry slowed to a hurried walk and tried to appear calm. It was no use, he had clearly been running. His breath burst from his throat in urgent draughts. His heart felt as if it might leap from his chest. Demetry wordlessly bustled by a group of students who had just been released from class.

"He came sprinting down the road like a madman," whispered one of the students, an older boy in his senior year of studies.

"It was that impish second year," said another, his voice edged with excitement. "He was running dead on Hanberg's heels. The lad looked terrified."

Demetry kept going.

Almost every building in the township — the dormitories, lecture halls, libraries, amphitheaters, and private lodgings — were lined one after the other along this central street. Most looked similar to the next — gray slate walls stacked a few stories high. Thatched roofs. Square windows. Narrow doors.

There was a face peering out through every window. No one was giving Demetry any heed — their eyes were directed further down the street, toward the headmaster's estate. Demetry tried to shrink into his cloak and appear inconspicuous as he shuffled toward that very same building.

"Blood," called one of the instructors from the shadows of her stoop. She was an old one-eyed seer. The crow she used for auguring cawed angrily upon her shoulder, snapping its beak.

Demetry looked down. The cuffs of his trousers were splattered with blood. He suddenly regretted venturing back into town. He could sense a crowd gathering to his rear, but he didn't dare look over his shoulder. Headmaster Rioley's estate was the next building on his right.

Just as Demetry reached the front step, there was a boom that caused the whole house to shudder on its foundation. Demetry suddenly felt as if a million needles were piercing his skin all at once. *Am I on fire?* He patted frantically over his body, beating at invisible flames. The pain dissipated as quickly as it began. It was as if his nerve endings had been scorched to their roots.

"There's no fire, so why do I feel this way?" he wondered aloud. On the periphery of his vision he saw a flicker of orange light in the second floor window. Flames. Joshua was burning.

Demetry gritted his teeth and rushed up the front steps. He plowed through the door — it was already ajar, hanging on a broken hinge. The foyer desk lay toppled over on its side, its contents strewn across the floor. Alongside the desk was a smear of blood. It was cast across the whitewashed walls and trailed up the stairs in great red droplets. The trail disappeared into the headmaster's bedroom. Demetry followed the path hesitantly, halting at the room's threshold. He was horrified by the prospect of what might await within. For a moment, he simply stared at the floor, collecting his resolve. Taking a deep breath, he peered within.

Gooseflesh shrouded his frame — his body reacting to the horror before his mind could comprehend what he was seeing. A writhing mound lay against the far wall, more black than red. It was Joshua. The boy's body resembled a roasted pig that had been left over the flames for too long. The room was filled with the odor of burnt flesh. Someone had struck Joshua with a pyromantic blast, shattering the bones in his arms, legs, and skull. Joshua's undead body mindlessly clawed at the floor, trying to worm his way forward, but his limbs were like jelly.

Laying opposite Joshua, in a heap of robes and fallen furniture, was the headmaster of the school. Headmaster Rioley was slumped over on his knees, his face pressed awkwardly into the wall. His body was half-buried beneath an overturned dresser. Half a dozen bloody circles pockmarked the headmaster's back. Stab wounds, Demetry surmised.

He was about to check for a pulse when a sputtering cough sounded near the door. Only then did Demetry realized Hanberg was also in the room. He was leaning against the wall behind the door. His fingertips resembled charcoal, singed from unleashing the spell that ravaged Joshua's body. His forearms were riddled with stab wounds, but more pressing were the wounds to his face and neck. One puncture wound was beneath his left eye, another a fingerbreath wide of his jugular. Hanberg was losing blood fast, but neither blow would prove fatal if tended to.

"You'll have to finish it yourself."

Demetry's eyes instinctively fell upon a length of honed steel that lay discarded beneath the headmaster's desk. How he knew it was there, he could not say. The weapon responsible for all of this havoc was nothing more than a letter opener.

Demetry tentatively picked up the blade and scuttled to Hanberg's side. Hanberg blinked in disbelief. "Murderer," he croaked. Demetry paid the accusation no mind. He opened Hanberg's cloak and tucked the *Paserani Haote* into a hidden pocket within the lining of the boy's cloak. Hanberg tried to remove the book from his pocket, but his hands were clumsy and weak. All he managed to do was put his own bloody fingerprints all over the book's cover.

Demetry felt along Hanberg's neck until he found the perfect spot just below the jawline; the artery throbbed beneath the pressure of his thumb. Satisfied he had the correct location, he pressed the tip of the blade to Hanberg's neck. Hanberg pawed at Demetry's arms, but his motions were without strength. Demetry gritted his teeth, building up the courage to do what needed to be done — to save his own life one more person had to die.

Three..., he counted off in head.

There was a crash in the foyer. Others were coming.

Two...

Boots thundered up the stairwell.

"One," Demetry said aloud.

Hanberg looked to him with pleading eyes, the

eyes of someone paralyzed by fear, the eyes of a child.

"Do it! Do it now!"

Demetry hesitated.

And that was how they found him, hands outstretched, letter opener held limply in an unsure grasp. One of the school elders shouldered Demetry out of the way and began to frantically tend to Hanberg's wounds. Another checked Headmaster Rioley for a pulse. No one approached Joshua's body — the scorched and blistered flesh was confirmation enough.

Demetry dropped the blade and sat cross-legged in the middle of the room. He rocked back and forth holding his head, wishing desperately he could wake up from this nightmare.

The elder tending to Hanberg held up the *Paserani Haote*, having discovered it in the boy's hidden pocket. The others nodded knowingly.

"Shep's hurt," Demetry vaguely heard himself say. "He's lying out there in the forest bleeding to death. You better hurry."

Firm hands grabbed either of his shoulders. Demetry let himself be led from the room.

"Do you know what they do to fools who perform necromancy?" whispered a voice in the recesses of Demetry's mind.

Demetry glanced over his shoulder, catching sight of Joshua's blackened body one last time. He was horrified to discover that the boy's scorched face was curled into a crispy grin.

CHAPTER
IV

PRISONS AND TOMBS

They hang men for the crime of necromancy. Hanberg's words repeated over and over in Demetry's head, like a refrain from a dark song. It served as a stark reminder of Demetry's fate.

So why am I still alive?

Demetry struggled to stay on his feet and keep walking, fearful of the repercussions if he stopped. He had never felt more tired in his life. Drained was the best way to describe it. Every muscle ached, and his head pounded with each heartbeat.

"Keep moving," hissed the guard to his rear. Demetry hadn't realized he had stopped. The prison guard tugged at the iron hoop cinched around Demetry's neck like a kennel master correcting a disobedient dog. Demetry almost lost his footing, caught himself, and continued on, shuffling down the dark corridor without complaint. Compliance was the best course of action — he learned that during his first few days of captivity. *I'm alive,* he kept telling himself. For now, that was good enough.

Justice had been swift. Demetry was in fetters before Headmaster Rioley's body was even cold. An emergency trial was held the next day. Hanberg testified against him. The boy's neck, face, and forearms were wrapped in bloody bandages. Every word Demetry spoke in his own defense was either shouted down or ignored. The school elders only needed a few minutes to deliberate. Demetry would be sent to the fortress prison of Coljack. Joshua's wraith body would be burned. For some reason Demetry felt worse about the second half of their decree. They had to wrap Joshua in chains to keep him from crawling out of the funerary pyre. Demetry never heard what happened to Shep. He could only pray that the big oaf was all right.

Demetry was bound hand and foot, like a pig made ready for slaughter, and carted off to Coljack. The men responsible for transporting Demetry to prison considered him a great deal more dangerous than he actually was. They shoved a horse bit into his mouth as soon as they left town, a precautionary measure, designed to keep Demetry from chanting a death spell. Not that he could perform such a spell even if he wanted. Demetry had never learned the words to a single offensive spell. Only apprentices learned such spells, and Demetry hadn't passed the rank of acolyte. He knew magic, yes, but he did not know how to use it as a weapon.

In the end, the horse bit served only as a cruel punishment. Demetry had to learn to drink without closing his mouth, to swallow gruel without chewing. The leather thong holding the bit in place chafed against his cheeks until his flesh was rubbed raw. Sleeping upright became his only option. Otherwise he would wake up with a blinding pain in his jaw. He had hoped that someone would remove the bit once he arrived to Coljack, but thus far no one seemed keen on showing him an ounce of mercy.

His escort consisted of three guards, a Yanish Brother, and the prison warden. They were touring Demetry about the grounds of the fortress prison as if he were a distinguished guest. Demetry hardly raised his eyes to take in the sights of his dreary new home — he was having a hard enough time not tripping over his own feet.

"Coljack was once a Wyrm fortress," explained the warden, leading the procession down a dark passage that seemed to go on forever. He had been prattling on about the history and lore of Coljack since Demetry arrived. "The fortress fell to the Throne of Caper during the War of Sundering and has been a prison ever since. Fortresses make convenient prisons — you only have to turn the locks around." He smiled at his own joke. No one else did, but the warden didn't seem to care.

"We've done our best to humanize the compound, but relics of the previous residents do remain." As he spoke, they reached a mosaic set in the wall that must have been a hundred paces in length. Images of winged men battling serpentine creatures were in one scene. The earth was cracked open like an egg in another. A third scene depicted a dozen glimmering stones wreathed in light. They were the fabled Guardian Stones, Demetry knew, ancient artifacts capable of reshaping the world. Here and there along the mosaic, hung tapestries displaying the white tower of the king. It was a vain effort to hide the most profane and sacrilegious images.

"The wealth of knowledge the Wyrm left behind within this building is astonishing," continued the warden. "The Library of Coljack was once one of the greatest repositories of books in the world. Of course, the most dangerous texts have been carted off to the capital. But the Arcane Council couldn't take everything. A man with your skill might find some of the volumes in our library truly enlightening. Once you are settled, I'll be certain to send a few books your way."

Demetry couldn't tell if it was a genuine offer or a trap. All Wyrm texts were forbidden, not just the *Paserani Haote*. Demetry decided it was best to remain quiet and keep his eyes focused on the floor.

As the warden spoke, Demetry couldn't help but feel that he had already met the man once before. The warden wore a short-trimmed beard in an effort to cover scarring on the left side of his face. His eyes were black-rimmed, sleep-deprived. His pale complexion made it obvious that he didn't spend much time outside. His left foot dragged behind him when he walked, and he leaned heavily upon a cane to compensate. A burgundy cape hung from his shoulders, the marking of a Capernican officer. Although the hem of his cape was stained with filth, the rest of his clothing was immaculate.

"Common criminals serve their terms here in the west wing," continued the warden. "While the elves are kept in the east wing." He pointed down a long corridor that disappeared into shadow. "A treaty with the Luthuanians dictates that the elves receive special treatment. Seems rather unfair, eh,

Sighelm?"

The Yanish Brother spit in the direction of the east wing. "A criminal is a criminal," said Sighelm. The man's gaunt face twisted into a scowl. "How can you ever repent and rediscover the majesty of the Guardians if you live a life of luxury?" Demetry had met more than a few Yanish Brothers in his life. Worshipers of the god-saint Yansarian, they toured the land trying to recruit disciples. Members were easy to spot — they all wore starched yellow robes and matching conical caps, and they all spouted the same nonsense about repentance and rebirth.

"Sighelm is our resident chaplain," said the Warden with a lopsided smirk. "My job is to keep the prisoners safe and securely locked away. Chaplain Sighelm's job is to liberate their souls."

"Are you a child of god?" asked Sighelm.

"I pray," garbled Demetry around the horse bit lodged in his mouth. "But the gods seem loath to answer."

The chaplain smirked. "In here, all men hear the voice of god eventually. Have faith, the weight on your soul will be lifted. You, too, will find liberation within these walls."

Seeing the disheveled state of the other prisoners caused Demetry to doubt that anyone's soul had been "liberated."

Arms snaked between iron bars as they walked through the corridor, grabbing at Demetry. The prisoners asked for food, begged for freedom, cried for mercy. The cells themselves were poorly lit, and Demetry saw little more than skeletal faces and grime-covered bodies. Toothless, filthy, and flea ridden, most of the prisoners wore unkempt beards. More than a few were balding from malnutrition. There was not a hopeful face among them. Demetry saw neither repentance nor reform, just desperation and agony.

"Is that why I'm still alive?" Demetry's words were almost unintelligible due to the horse bit. "Am I here to repent my sins?"

The warden motioned for the guards to stop. "You've worn that thing long enough, don't you think?" He unfastened the leather thong and removed the bit. Demetry had never known such relief in his entire life.

"Thank you." It was the first time Demetry was able to speak freely in over a month. His voice sounded odd, almost not his own. His tongue felt clumsy and swollen.

"Common men fear what they don't understand," said the warden, giving Demetry's shoulder a friendly pat. "They fear men like us almost as much as they fear the gods."

"You're a magic?" asked Demetry. He rubbed at his jaw, trying to massage away the pain.

"Not exactly," said the warden. "You don't remember me, do you?" He shrugged. "In truth, I'm not surprised. I was in my senior year of studies when they brought you into the headmaster's quarters." He flattened his hand to waist level to illustrate Demetry's height at the time. "You were a small lad, not a day past your fourth birthday if I recall."

"I'm sorry, I don't remember you."

"Cendrik Carveth," announced the warden, his voice baring a degree of pride. The Carveth family owned a fleet of trading vessels that hailed out of Orith, Demetry recalled. They weren't exactly nobility, but they weren't paupers either. Demetry wondered who Cendrik had pissed off to get stationed here.

"I had a class with a Jory Carveth," said Demetry, feeling a degree of excitement. Having a connection to the warden might be quite beneficial in this abysmal setting. "Any relation?"

"Jory is my cousin. Now there's a wispy little brat. I'd tell you to wish him well, but it's not likely you two will ever cross paths." He laughed at that. His guards forced a snicker. Sighelm frowned — he seemed to do that most of the time. Demetry gave his best false smile, eager not to offend.

Warden Cendrik waved them onward. In case Demetry missed the point, Chaplain Sighelm yanked on the iron collar the guards had locked around Demetry's neck when he first arrived. The collar bit harshly into Demetry's neck, causing him to cry out in pain. The warden completely ignored the abuse. That was a troubling sign.

"We keep men of the more dangerous variety underground," continued Warden Cendrik as they descended a flight of stair. "Dark children and magics, mostly. Criminals with the greatest propensity to escape. Security is my utmost priority."

The blood-curdling cries of madmen wafted down from the upper levels, and still they went deeper. They entered a cell block that looked more like an abandoned mineshaft than a prison block. Torches lined the walls, but not a single one was lit.

"Demetry, why don't you do us a favor and illuminate the path."

Demetry gave Warden Cendrik a confused look.

"Use your magic, with my blessing of course." Cendrik bowed and stepped out of the way.

Bringing light to an unlit torch was easy enough, Demetry had been able to do it since his first year at Taper. He knew half a dozen illumination spells that would suffice. He chose one that was notably complex, hoping to impress Cendrik with his skills. "*Missat majrl re hesi palrir.*"

Nothing happened.

Cendrik laughed. "I guess you haven't figured out why I've trusted you without a gag." He gave Demetry's collar a gentle shake. There was something dull and pointed set into the back of the collar that Demetry hadn't noticed before.

"It's a Sundering Stone, in case you're wondering," said Cendrik, his white teeth showing in the dark. Demetry had learned about the magical stones in his studies. Rarer than rubies, harder than diamonds, worth more than gold. The stones had a single useful attribute, they drained away one's magical vitality. They were rumored to have once been used as weapons against the gods.

"You've gelded me."

"We've made you mortal," said Chaplain Sighelm. "How can you repent when the power of the gods is at your fingertips?"

Demetry thought he might be sick.

"Don't worry," said Cendrik. "The results are temporary. Your powers will return in due time. Like I said, security is my utmost priority. You killed the headmaster of Taper, or don't you recall."

Demetry lowered his eyes. "It was a mistake."

Sighelm snorted and glared at Demetry, his weasel face full of hatred. "Dead is dead, mistake or not. The first step toward repentance is accepting the blame."

Cendrik gestured for the guard carrying a torch to illuminate the path. They followed closed behind.

"Now don't get me wrong," continued Cendrik, hobbling after the torchbearer. "I never really liked Headmaster Rioley. A true bastard, that one. He's the reason I'm here whiling away in a prison full of cutthroats and lunatics. He wouldn't recommend me to the Academy Arcanum. Claimed I lacked the talent. In truth, it was the noble pedigree I lacked. Wrong parents. Wrong blood. Wrong connections." He smirked. "In a way, you and I are both prisoners here."

They stopped before a wooden door reinforced with metal banding. A small square gap was cut out of the bottom of the door, large enough for a waste pail to pass through, but not much else.

The first inklings of fear entered Demetry's heart. He had spent all of his time and energy since the incident simply trying to survive. Little thought had gone into how his life would be once he arrived to Coljack.

"*Death can be merciful*," whispered a voice within the recesses of his mind. Demetry snorted, unwilling to accept the bitter conclusion. Admittedly, the prison cell lying before him was little better than an empty grave, but as long as he was alive, there was hope. He would have to remember that in the days and weeks ahead — nothing would be easy from this point forward.

The guards removed the collar from around Demetry's neck, allowing him to see the blue-green Sundering Stone set in the back of the collar. The gem glowed brightly with the magical energy it had absorbed from Demetry's body.

"Why didn't the Arcane Council condemn me to death?" asked Demetry.

"Because death wasn't part of the Weaver's plan," said Cendrik matter-of-factly. He smiled. "I've always felt a certain connection with my magic guests. Given our history, I think you and I are going to be especially close."

Sighelm unlocked the cell door. He had to strain to pry it open; the hinges squealed in protest. The black cell opened before Demetry like a gaping maw.

"*Don't go in there*," urged a voice in his head. "*You'll never come out. No one ever comes out...*"

Demetry suddenly felt short of breath. He could

feel the blood drain from his face. "No, wait. I can't breathe. I..." Demetry tried to resist, but firm hands latched onto either of his shoulders, inching him toward the door. A boot struck him in the small of his back and he tumbled into the cell, landing on his hands and knees. The door clacked shut behind him.

Demetry had only a split second to take in his surroundings. Four walls, all damp and stained green. The floor was an uneven slap of rock little more than two spans square. The reek of urine was so strong it stung his eyes. In the far corner, seated atop a pile of a hay was a hulking figure, bald-headed, front teeth missing, pale eyes glaring angrily.

Demetry gasped.

The torch outside his cell was extinguished.

"Oh. Make sure to say hello to your cellmate," called Cendrik from beyond the door. His voice and footsteps faded into the distance. "Clyde is his name. He mostly grunts and growls. Lost his tongue for telling too many fibs. Good old Lying Clyde. A bit irritable, that one. You two have fun. I'll check on you in a few days. If you need anything, just let me know." Cendrik whistled merrily as he walked away.

Demetry had never known such darkness. The

heavy breathing of his cellmate seemed to thunder in the space. The hay rustled as Clyde shifted atop the mound. The beat of his own heart thudded in Demetry's ear. He needed light.

"*Missat majrl re hesi palrir,*" whispered Demetry. Nothing.

"*Missat majrl re hesi palrir.*" Darkness remained.

"*Missat majrl re hesi palrir.*" The torch outside his room crackled to life, dimly illuminating the space through the flap in the bottom of the door. Clyde was still seated in the corner, still breathing through his mouth like every breath was a chore, still glaring at Demetry with eyes full of rage.

Demetry tried not to let fear get the better of him. "I'm Demetry," he managed, his voice a mere squeak.

Clyde sat proudly atop his pile of straw like a king upon a throne. *A very filthy king, that is,* thought Demetry. The wool shirt and pants worn by the man were riddled with holes and stained with night soil. Demetry imagined he would soon look the same.

Clyde jabbed Demetry in the chest and then pointed to the filth ridden corner opposite the hay pile. "*Yours,*" he garbled from his tongueless mouth. "*Mine.*" He patting the pile of hay. The words were nearly unintelligible, but Demetry got the point.

He slunk to the corner Clyde had designated as his, feeling suddenly envious of the time when Shep was the scariest person he encountered in his day-to-day life. He let the torch in the corridor gutter to darkness, deciding it was best not to draw the attention of the guards. The last thing Demetry saw before darkness engulfed the cell was Clyde, staring at him and licking his lips.

• • •

"Flee. Flee now!"

The disembodied voice echoed through the empty forests.

Demetry's eyes darted to and fro, searching for the speaker. "Where are you?" he called. The ceaseless babble of the nearby stream was the only reply.

I'm alone, he realized. Hanberg was gone, as were Joshua and Shep. Demetry was free to set his own fate without having to fear that someone might intervene. All he had to do was cross the stream and venture north. He could leave his old life behind and start over, free from the weight of his past sins. One foot in front of the other — that was all it took. He breathed deep and stepped into the stream.

Somewhere in the woods Shep screamed, a pitiful cry full of desperation and fear. Demetry didn't turn back. He trudged onward into the stream. The rushing water rose to his knees, then his thighs, then his waist. The stream was deeper than he imagined, but he would not be deterred.

The water splashed behind him. Demetry was not alone. Joshua trailed in his wake stabbing at the water with a letter opener. The orphan boy was desperately trying to turn back the rising current with his feeble blade. It was no use — the current was rising. Headmaster Rioley's limp body came bobbing down the stream. Demetry tried to ignore the stab wounds in the headmaster's back, but his eyes were drawn to the blood. The laugh of a madman sounded on the far bank. Demetry discovered Shep standing there. He was pointing and laughing, but his face was twisted in a grimace. The water rose higher. To Demetry's chest. To his neck.

"I can't swim," cried Demetry as the water lapped at his chin. He lost contact with the stream bed, his feet floundering in the depths. He beat his arms against the water, desperately trying to stay afloat. "Please! Somebody help me!"

Joshua was eager to assist. He leapt on Demetry's back and forced his head beneath the waves. Headmaster Rioley joined in, and together they pulled Demetry deeper and deeper into the depths. Demetry's world became shades of black, shadows upon shadows. Demetry's body began to spasm, his strength ebbing fast. He couldn't hold his breath forever.

"Why don't you just swallow water and kill yourself," he heard Shep say, as the boy's bloated body washed by in the current.

Shep was right, Demetry was only avoiding the inevitable. There was nowhere else for him to go. He breathed in deep, feeling the sting of water fill his nostrils, his mouth, his throat. The water was warm and tasted sour. He coughed and spasmed, his lungs inadvertently drawing in more water as they desperately sought out air. And all this while someone was laughing, a guttural broken laugh that wracked at the nerves.

Demetry opened his eyes to discover he was lying face down in an ever-growing puddle of piss. A deep throated sound that might have been a laugh echoed in the small prison cell. Clyde was standing over him, his legs straddling Demetry's body. The man was peeing on the hinges to the cell door — drenching Demetry was just a happy byproduct.

Demetry scurried to his feet, frantically wiping at

his face with disgust. He was horrified to discover his chest and sleeves were drenched as well. Demetry gagged, and would have likely thrown up had he any food in his stomach.

Clyde laced up his breeches and returned to his pile of hay as if nothing had happened.

One look at the cell door made it clear that this wasn't Clyde's first time performing the deed — the metal hinges were badly corroded, and the wooden frame was beginning to fail. Demetry almost had to admire the will power it took to pee on the same hinges day after day, month after month, year after year with the hope of one day breaking down the door. Almost.

He was just beginning to conjure up the courage to say something when a bucket of pale gruel slid through the flap at the base of the door. Clyde was on the gruel before Demetry could take a step toward the bucket. He slurped it down in hungry gulps, not bothering to chew. Within a few second he had downed most of the pail.

"Wait a second, some of that's mine!" cried Demetry, reaching for the pail.

Clyde backhanded Demetry so hard it felt as if he had been struck in the face with a cudgel. He fell flat on his back, his left ear screaming in pain. His cheek was lacerated just beneath the eye. Clyde tossed the bucket on Demetry and what little gruel remained spilled down his chest. Clyde muttered something unintelligible, but Demetry got the point; Clyde had first dibs on food. Always.

Demetry wiped the food off his chest, letting it splatter onto the floor. He spent the rest of the day fuming in the corner and nursing his injured jaw — not that this bothered Clyde one bit. The evening feeding went much the same way, only this time Clyde overturned the bucket on Demetry's head.

Demetry went to bed furious and starving, but the hollow ache in his stomach kept slumber at bay. Finally, his hunger defeated his pride. When he was certain Clyde was asleep, Demetry crawled over to the pile of discarded slop that lay heaped on the floor and shoveled it into his mouth. The gruel had a foul taste, but that didn't stop him from forcing down every last bit. A few hours later, Demetry woke up feeling like there were mice trying to chew through his intestines. He promptly threw up every ounce of food in his stomach.

CHAPTER
V

THE OLD AND THE NEW

Demetry edged to the door, slithering along on his stomach until his eyes drew flush with the threshold. He was careful not to wake Clyde. The ogre of a man lay atop his pile of hay snoring loudly; that was the one sound the man was more than capable of making.

Demetry slowly drew back the flap on the base of the door. The hinge squealed. Clyde snorted, his snoring ceased. Demetry's breath caught in his throat. An involuntary shiver pimpled his skin. He peered over his shoulder, fearful he had awakened Clyde from his slumber. Clyde scratched at a scab on his forearm, readjusted his body atop his pile of hay, and promptly resumed snoring. Demetry exhaled with relief and resumed his vigil staring into the corridor beyond the cell door.

A sliver of torchlight illuminated the walkway.

The guards were making their rounds. A furry shape preceded the reach of the torchlight, scampering down the passage on all fours with its body pressed against the far wall. It was a rat — Demetry's rat to be more precise. The rat stopped periodically to raise its nose and sniff at the air, before scurrying forward a few more feet and repeating the process all over again. The rat was a curiously cautious creature, even in death.

Demetry reached out into the corridor and motioned for the critter. The rat obediently crawled atop Demetry's outstretched palm and immediately went limp. Demetry stroked the rat's black body. The rat didn't blink, didn't twitch, didn't breathe. To an outside observer, the rat was dead. But she was so much more than that. He called her Sneak, a suitable name given her purpose. He tucked the rat in his pocket, worried that Clyde might awaken and discover him stroking a dead rat; there was no telling how Clyde would react.

The rat was a gift from Clyde. A few weeks earlier, instead of sharing the evening bucket of gruel, Clyde decided to eat both portions. When Demetry complained of hunger, Clyde rummaged through his pile of hay and produced the carcass of a long dead rat. He threw the rotten carcass at Demetry. Blinded by his hunger, Demetry almost took a bite, but at the last second an idea entered his head. To a necromancer, a dead rat could be much more than a desperate meal.

Sneak became Demetry's eyes and ears in Coljack. He had to make sure she avoided the kennel and the pair of tomcats that prowled the upper floors, but other than that, she could pass freely through the halls of the fortress prison without the guards or prisoners giving her any mind.

Demetry's ability to control the undead creature was quickly improving. He could feel the link between his subconscious thoughts and the rat's actions growing stronger by the day. Sometimes, while he slept, he would dream of walking the halls of Coljack. When he woke up, he would discover that Sneak was gone. With keen focus he could get her to carry out simple tasks — fetch a piece of bread from the larder, explore the upper levels of the prison, find Warden Cendrik's private chambers, search for a way out. Sometimes Sneak complied, at other times he seemed to lose all control of her. The rat would revert to a state in which she acted on pure instinct. She would seek out food, skirt from sudden noises, or hide in the darkest corner of the room. Such actions left Demetry to wonder if an echo of Sneak's old consciousness remained.

What's dead is dead, he often reminded himself. He would not allow himself to feel guilty for reanimating rotten flesh that would have otherwise turned to dust. Besides, Sneak was proving an invaluable asset. The rat provided Demetry with glimpses of a world he could not visit himself.

Coljack was a vast complex, much larger than the weathered fortress and collection of derelict outbuildings Demetry had seen when he first arrived. There were levels below Demetry's cell that delved deep into the earth — snaking tunnels with forks aplenty and rickety lifts that lowered into abyssal pits. There were doors inscribed with protective wards, stone tombs untouched by light, and at the deepest levels, the chime of working hammers.

Sneak's discoveries were all very intriguing, but in truth, it was really just a way to pass the time. Sneak couldn't unlock the door to Demetry's cell — he tried that already. And she couldn't chew through the wooden door — her front incisors were already worn down to useless nubs. In truth, walking the dark corridors of Coljack was really just a way for Demetry to avoid the crushing monotony of prison life.

The pad of steel-toed boots sounded in the

corridor. *Right on time,* thought Demetry, as he settled back into his corner and waited.

Life within the cell followed a numbing routine. Shiver at night. Breakfast at dawn. Go mad with boredom during the day. Dinner at dusk if Clyde felt like sharing. Try to ignore the nagging voices that resounded in his head all the time.

"I'm as much a prisoner here as you are." The voice in Demetry's head sounded much too similar to Joshua for Demetry's liking. He shifted uncomfortably and punched at his brow with the flat of his hand, trying to drive the whining voice into silence. The voice only intensified.

"Why are we here, Demetry? The punishment for necromancy is death, yet someone has decided to keep you alive. Why is that?"

"I'm supposed to repent and reform," muttered Demetry, repeating Warden Cendrik words.

"You don't actually believe that."

The voice was right, Demetry had his doubts. On sleepless nights he toyed with thoughts of remorse, wondering if salvation could be achieved if he repented for his past sins. But what did repentance even look like? Regret. Sorrow. Acceptance of blame. Try as he might, Demetry found himself drawing short of such feelings. He truly did feel awful about Headmaster Rioley's death, and he regretted not stopping to aid Shep in the woods. But why should he feel remorse over someone else's actions? Joshua was the one at fault. Joshua was responsible for destroying Demetry's life — first by getting himself killed and then by going on a murderous rampage.

"Headmaster Rioley deserved to die," whispered the voice in reply. *"Shep deserved to die. Hanberg deserved to die. Blowhards, fools, and bullies. They all deserved to die."*

Demetry shook the discordant thought from his head. They deserved to die no more than Demetry deserved to live the rest of his life in this dungeon.

If Demetry felt regret over anything, it would be that he didn't flee north while he had the chance. Joshua's rampage was the opening he needed to slip away. That was the single greatest mistake of Demetry's life. If such an opportunity arose again, he would not flinch, he would not falter, he would act, consequences to others be damned.

Demetry was so caught up in his own thoughts that he did not notice a guard had stopped outside his cell door. A slop pail slid through the flap in the door and the guard moved on. It was filled to the brim with pale gray sludge. Despite the grumble of his stomach, Demetry kept his distance from the food. He knew better than to eat any without his cellmate's permission. Clyde always got first dibs on food. It was one of Clyde's five rules. The others — stay off the hay, piss on the hinges, shit in the bucket, and never ever bother a sleeping Clyde. Demetry had learned each of Clyde's rules the hard way.

Not keen on adding to the collage of bruises that covered his back, Demetry crouched in the corner and waited. Clyde would eventually wake up and eat his fill. Demetry would be free to eat whatever dregs remained. An unfair arrangement in an unfair world, but what was Demetry to do? Clyde was a head taller than Demetry, and a great deal stronger. Stubbornness and feigned ignorance had only bought Demetry pain.

"So what is compliance buying you?"

"A slow death," Demetry muttered. He was unable to ignore the reality that was staring back at him every time he glimpsed his own reflection in a pail of water.

His health was deteriorating fast. By the end of the first month, his clothes ceased fitting properly. By the end of the second month, he could feel the divots between every rib in his chest. By the end of the third month, he ran out of notches on his belt. Unable to cinch his belt any tighter, he tied the loose ends in a knot around his shrunken waist.

Whatever strength he once had was long gone.

The knobby joints of his knees periodically gave out when he tried to move, and if he stood too fast he risked passing out. There were days when he didn't even bother to stand. When he ran his hand over his lice-ridden scalp, hair came out in chunks. His teeth were loose in his gums. His vision seemed to be worsening as well — sometimes Clyde was no more than an indistinct blob seated atop his throne of hay.

Was this the penitence that Chaplain Sighelm spoke about so fondly? Demetry shook his head. "There's no penitence here, just misery and suffering." Demetry was so tired and sick that he didn't care that he was talking to himself. "Perhaps this was what the elder council truly wanted. Death was too merciful a punishment for my crime. I'm damned."

Footsteps sounded in the corridor. A second bucket slid under the door. Demetry blinked in disbelief. The first bucket still stood there, untouched.

Had the guards made a mistake? Perhaps Demetry had passed out and lost track of time — it wouldn't have been the first time that happened. Clyde stirred from his slumber, roused by the chime of voices in the hall.

Demetry looked at the two buckets, each filled

nearly to the brim. It was a feast; there was more than enough gruel for them both to eat their fill. Demetry edged as close to the bucket as he would dare. He looked to Clyde with pleading eyes.

Clyde shoved Demetry to the floor and stepped over him to get to the food. He returned to his throne of hay, greedily clutching a bucket in each hand. He devoured the first serving in record time and then went straight into the second pail without taking a break. Demetry gaped in disbelief as Clyde slurped down the food. He clearly had no intention to share.

Demetry was tempted to attack Clyde, to try to wrestle the slop bucket from his grasp before the last bit passed his lips, but he knew it would be a losing battle. Demetry might have had a chance when they first locked him in the cell, but now he was just skin and bones.

"Please, I'm starving." Demetry was embarrassed by the frailness of his voice. A sound passed Clyde's lips that might have been a laugh.

More footsteps in the corridor. The guard was returning, having completed his rounds.

Demetry crawled to the door, placing his lips to the flap.

"Please, I need food!" The words squeaked from his mouth. There was silence in the corridor. He was unsure if anyone was still out there, if anyone cared, if anyone would reply. "Warden Cendrik told me to call for him if I needed help. Please, fetch me the warden!"

A pair of boots clacked to a halt on the far side of the door. The hem of a dirty yellow robe lay just on the periphery of Demetry's vision. A Yanish Brother.

"I need help." This time, Demetry's voice sounded weak, his request hollow. He had overheard the Yanish Brothers "helping" other inmates. It usually involved a flail.

Not surprisingly, the Yanish Brother did not reply. For a while he simply stood there, unmoving. The lock on the door slowly turned over. Clyde whimpered, the first sign that something was wrong. Demetry edged away from the door, his hope turning to fear.

The door swung open, groaning on its corroded hinges. A yellow-robed figure strode into the room. It was Chaplain Sighelm. The weasel-faced man stood in the doorway and slowly surveyed the cell. He spotted Clyde first and his lips stiffened into a grim frown. A wooden club rested in Chaplain Sighelm's hand.

The chaplain lunged toward Clyde, swinging the club like a man cleaving firewood. Clyde threw his arms over his head just as Sighelm struck. There was a crack and a pitiful cry as Clyde's arm broke at the wrist. Sighelm turned his attention to Demetry. Demetry didn't even bother to raise his hands in defense, he simply sat there in stunned silence and took the club square in the jaw.

Darkness ensued.

•   •   •

Demetry awoke to a merry whistle.

"I heard you were asking for me," said Warden Cendrik. All Demetry could see of the warden was a pair of impeccably polished black leather boots and the tip of his wooden cane. Demetry was lying on a table, his stomach pressed flat against the coarse hard wood, his face dangling over the edge.

"You should have called for me sooner," continued the warden. "Time has not been kind to you." He gave Demetry's back a reassuring pat.

A Yanish Brother stood beside the table working at Demetry's belt while another tried to strip off Demetry's shirt.

"Just cut the rags off of him," called a shrill voice. It was Chaplain Sighelm. There was a swishing noise, the sound of shears cutting through fabric, and Demetry's tattered clothes were stripped away. Gooseflesh shrouded Demetry's naked frame.

"I want those lice-ridden rags thrown in the fire," instructed Warden Cendrik. He lifted Demetry's chin and turned his head from side to side, inspecting the wound on Demetry's brow. "The chaplain got you good. Lucky he didn't break your skull. I always tell him not to use the club. Sighelm has a tendency to get carried away." Cendrik probed the wound with his finger, causing a blinding pain to flash through Demetry's head. "You'll need stitches, I fear."

"I... I haven't eaten in a few days," managed Demetry. He was suddenly self-aware of his state, embarrassed even. His clothes were soiled with filth, pus, and piss. He had gone half-bald, and his teeth were rotting out of his head. He tried to cover his mouth with his palm, but found he couldn't draw his hand to his mouth.

"Don't try to move too much," said Cendrik, more an order than advice. "You're in fetters. It'll keep you from thrashing around too much once the trial begins. I don't want you to hurt yourself."

Demetry tried to lift his arms and legs. When that didn't work he tried to turn over on his back. He was held fast by leather bindings cinched around his ankles and wrists.

"My trial? What's happening? What are you

doing?" A cold panic seized him. He pulled against his bindings to no avail. One of the Yanish Brothers cinched his wrist bindings even tighter. "Take me back to my cell. I want to go back."

"There's something in his pocket," reported a guard that was rummaging through Demetry's clothes. The guard's face curled with disgust as he held up Sneak by her tail. "He's a sick one. It's a dead rat."

Sneak's body suddenly sprung life, her legs kicking wildly. She swung like a pendulum in the man's grasp and managed to lock her nubby jaws around the guard's wrist. There was a flash of red, and the guard howled in surprise. He flung Sneak across the room. The rat hit the ground running, and before anyone could react she darted from the room.

"Get me that rat," ordered Cendrik.

The guard looked as if he might object, then thought better of it. Clutching his bleeding wrist, he ran after the rodent. Demetry was quite certain Sneak would not be caught.

Cendrik drew his face level with Demetry's eyes. "Made yourself a friend, I see. Have you forgotten that necromancy is a sin? Chaplain Sighelm doesn't take kindly to such dark transgressions." He was smiling from ear to ear.

Light flared as Demetry's clothes were deposited in the fireplace, briefly illuminating the room in full. Examination tables were lined in neat rows, while fetters and chains, hooks and pincers, choke pears and iron masks, hung on the far wall. He was in a part of Coljack he had never seen before, deep down or high up. He couldn't be sure.

"You're in the Tower of Repentance," said Sighelm, coming to stand beside Demetry's body. "Once the trial begins, it is best that the other prisoners hear your cries of penance. Forgiveness comes to those who openly and honestly beg the gods."

"I beg the gods for forgiveness," declared Demetry in his loudest voice.

Sighelm snorted. "Without pain, how can we know you're being sincere."

Demetry's stomach lurched as the table suddenly spun on a set of hinges. He was hoisted upright, his face drawing level with the warden's.

"Calm, Demetry, be calm." Cendrik gave Demetry's shoulder a reassuring squeeze. "We're old chums from school. I wouldn't do anything that would cause you permanent harm. We're going to put you through a few tests, that's all." Steel clattered just outside of Demetry's view as the Yanish Brothers made preparations. Images of razors and curved knives, saw blades and pincers blossomed in Demetry's mind. His body broke out in a cold sweat.

There was a sharp crack as Chaplain Sighelm snapped a whip in the air.

Demetry felt like his heart might leap from his chest. "Warden, please. I'm tired and hungry and weak. I..."

Cendrik waved off his plea. "We had to wait until you were desperate, your body beaten down, your spirit dwindling. Only then would your will to survive be most instinctual." He shook his head. "I apologize ahead of time — this test will seem cruel. But when we are finished, you will be reborn."

The whip cracked again, this time coming so close it moved the hairs on Demetry's head.

"Please..."

"You must open yourself to the void. You must save yourself with your magic."

"I was only an acolyte. I never learned how to defend myself with magic. I don't know the words to the spells. Please, you don't understand."

Cendrik's face softened, and for a second Demetry thought he finally understood. "You're mistaken, Demetry. Words won't save you." He lodged the sour tasting horse bit into Demetry's mouth, cinching tight the leather thong that held it in place. "The gods taught men how to use words to weave spells, but there is an older magic that lies dormant in a blessed few." He tapped Demetry's forehead. "The Old Magic is the magic of the mind. You don't need to know the words. Just focus and it will be. Deliverance comes to those who ask. Use the Old Magic, Demetry. Embrace your rebirth."

The Old Magic was akin to a force of nature, destructive and uncontrollable. It was once heralded as the great equalizer between gods and men, but only the most foolhardy of magics attempted to master the perilous power. Some children were born with the ability to manipulate the Old Magic, but by the time they learned to talk, the gift would vanish. The teachers at Taper purposefully avoided the topic, fearful that they might accidentally awaken the latent power in one of their students. Even Demetry knew better than to dabble in such dark and dangerous arts. "Why do you think I know how to use the Old Magic?" Demetry tried to scream. The words came out muffled and incomprehensible.

"Because you are a necromancer. Because you used a spell from the Paserani Haote," whispered the voice in Demetry's head.

There it was, the root of this whole

misunderstanding. The *Paserani Haote* contained numerous passages concerning the Old Magic. How to channel the Sundered Soul, how to maintain the void, how to focus one's mind to prevent accidental outcomes. The one thing the book didn't mention was how to access the Old Magic itself. Demetry mostly skimmed over these parts. He was more interested in the alternate histories written in the book that were not attainable anywhere else. That, and the forbidden New Magic spells contained in the back of the book.

A new fear entered Demetry's heart, greater than his fear of torture, and whips, and gushing wounds. They had kept him alive because they thought he could manipulate the Old Magic. *What will happen when they discover I can't?*

Demetry shook his head, his eyes pleading for Cendrik to stop, to delay, to give him more time to prepare.

Cendrik's face was impassive. He nodded to the chaplain. "Chaplain Sighelm, if you will."

The whip snapped, this time making sharp contact with the small of Demetry's back. It was like being kicked by a mule. Before his mind could fully process the pain the whip snapped again, this time cleaving his right shoulder blade. Demetry champed down so hard on the horse bit he thought it might break in two. The third blow struck square down the length of his spine. The fourth blow licked over his shoulder and lacerated his chest.

Demetry lost count of how many times they whipped him. Each strike was like a bolt of lightning, deafening to the ears. The pain was crippling. He felt his stomach turn over, and the meager contents of his stomach surged up his throat and came dribbling from his lips.

Warden Cendrik stood across from him, his face only a few inches away, his eyes hopeful, his mouth parted with excitement, as if at any moment something miraculous might occur. "Channel the Sundered Soul," whispered Cendrik. "Envision the void and it will be."

Demetry envisioned nothing but his scoured and bleeding back. He wondered what he could do, if anything, to make the torture end. The Old Magic was beyond him — beyond the reach of anyone, save untrained toddlers and street waifs like Joshua. The ability to master the power had vanished with the Sundering of the Gods. Why did this fool believe that pain, fear, and desperation could change any of that?

Warden Cendrik was not deterred. He motioned for Chaplain Sighelm to keep at it. Steel clattered behind Demetry, and suddenly a scalpel was shoved before Demetry's left eye, a guttering torch before the right. "Do you want the blade or the fire?"

Demetry didn't answer. He was too scared to even think about which was worse.

Chaplain Sighelm chose the scalpel. He drew the blade from Demetry's brow to the base of his neck. The pain registered a moment later, followed shortly thereafter by blood. It cascaded across his eyes, blurring his vision. It trickled down his back, around his buttocks, down the backs of his legs, dripping from his toes. A red pool began to form on the floor.

"A man can lose a quarter of his blood before succumbing to his wounds," whispered Sighelm into his ear. "How much do you suppose you've lost?"

Demetry stared at the growing puddle, aghast. He felt his skin turn waxen. His body felt cold. Demetry's head lolled, his consciousness ebbed.

Still, Warden Cendrik appeared hopeful. He smacked Demetry in the face. "Stay with me. Focus. Heal your wounds. Stop the bleeding. Save yourself."

"I can't," Demetry moaned around the horse bit, the blood bubbling on his lips.

"You can. You will. You must."

A noose looped around Demetry's throat and Chaplain Sighelm yanked it tight.

"Stop him Demetry. Use your magic," screamed the warden, his voice now twinged with desperation. "Become one with the Shadow. Channel the Sundered Soul. Do it. Do it now!"

Demetry tried to reply, but his voice only crackled in his throat, a pitiful death rattle. Demetry eyes rolled back in his head as the noose cinched tighter and tighter. His limbs clattered useless against the table. A black creeping haze seemed to be encroaching from all sides, spilling across the floor, clambering up the walls, reaching across the ceiling. *They're going to kill me,* he realized with stark certainty.

"It's not so bad," whispered a faceless voice. *"Just let yourself fade. Fade. Fade..."*

The voice was right. The oblivion of the afterworld seemed a great deal better than a lifetime of torture and imprisonment. Demetry stopped trying to resist and embraced the end.

Warden Cendrik's ecstasy turned to disappointment as he saw Demetry surrender to Fate. His lips curled in a pout. "I thought you were the one." He shook his head and motioned for Sighelm to stop. The pressure on the noose slackened.

Demetry's airway reopened. It burned like fire to breathe, but he did so anyway, taking in long desperate draughts. It felt like someone had taken a cheese grater to the inside of his throat. His cheeks tickled and burned as the blood came rushing back. His vision slowly cleared.

Warden Cendrik shook his head with disappointment and turned his back on Demetry. "Patch him up and return him to his cell. We'll try again in a few weeks."

Chaplain Sighelm threw down the noose with disgust and followed after the warden.

Demetry was so beaten and bloodied he scarcely felt relief that he was still alive. When they unfastened the fetters holding Demetry to the table he collapsed to the floor, coming to rest in a puddle of his own blood.

The guards had to carry Demetry through the corridors, his feet dragging limply in his wake. They didn't even bother with the gelding collar — Demetry was a threat to no one in his current state. They unceremoniously tossed Demetry inside his cell, locked the door, and walked away.

Demetry would have gladly laid there for the rest of eternity, but Clyde had different plans.

"*I kill you*," screeched Clyde. It was the most

comprehensible thing Demetry had ever heard the man utter.

Demetry's mind flared to sudden wakefulness, but it was already too late. Clyde landed on top of Demetry's chest, knocking the air from his lungs. Before he knew what was happening, Demetry's arms were pinned beneath Clyde's legs. The man was in an inconsolable rage. One look at Clyde's left arm explained why. His forearm was broken. The splintered bone caused the skin to bulge grotesquely. Sighelm had inflicted the ghastly injury with his club, but it was clear who Clyde blamed.

"I'm sorry," blurted Demetry. His voice was a mere squeak.

Clyde grabbed a handful of hay and shoved it into Demetry's mouth as he apologized. Demetry tried to tongue the foul tasting hay out of his mouth only for Clyde to jam a second handful in. Demetry gagged on the hay, inadvertently drawing it back toward his throat. Another handful prevented him from being able to close his mouth, a fourth clogged his airway. Clyde pinched Demetry's nose shut with his good hand. He grinned wickedly, his intention clear.

Demetry couldn't get his hands free. He couldn't clear his throat. He couldn't breathe. This was not Warden Cendrik's test. Clyde wasn't going to stop at the last second. Clyde was actually going to kill him.

Demetry managed to wiggle one arm free and tried to push Clyde off, but the man was too strong. Demetry searched for a weapon. The slop pail was toppled over on its side only a few feet away. If he could reach the pail he might be able to club Clyde in the head. That might stun Clyde long enough for Demetry to clear his throat. Demetry reached for the handle, his fingers twitching as they fell just short. Another inch, Demetry needed just one more inch.

The slop pail began to rattle and shake, some invisible force acting upon the inanimate object. Demetry's eyes flared wide with shock. The pail suddenly lurched into motion, flying through the air at a speed that was nearly impossible to follow. It slammed into Clyde's lower jaw, the mouth of the pail scooping off the bottom half of Clyde's face without losing an ounce of momentum. The pail crashed into the far wall, carrying its macabre payload with it. What was left of Clyde's face was a red mess. Clyde pawed at his missing jaw in stunned horror.

Demetry was almost as stunned as Clyde, but he did not have time to waste.

"*Get him off of you!*" screamed a disembodied

voice.

An invisible force seized Clyde by the base of the skull, yanking him off of Demetry's chest and into the air. Clyde flew headfirst into the cell door, the top of his brow striking the unyielding wood like a battering ram. There came a sickening crack and the door gave way.

Demetry rolled over and vomited up the hay. He was too stunned to think straight. What force had sent the pail slicing through Clyde's face? What force had seized Clyde and sent him hurtling through the air? Demetry's eyes wandered to Clyde's body and the ruined door. Everything about the scene was impossible and absurd. He couldn't stop a maniacal snicker from passing his lips. "Look, Clyde, you finally broke down the door."

Clyde didn't answer, and from the look of his caved-in skull he never would.

Demetry was still picking strands of hay out of his mouth when a low whistle sounded down the corridor. Warden Cendrik stepped out of the gloom, giving Demetry a congratulatory *tap*, *tap*, *tap*, with the tip of his cane. "I knew the blood of the old gods courses through your veins. The Guardians be praised!" Cendrik crossed himself in the gesture of the faithful.

Demetry remained on the ground, still too weak to stand. His eyes slowly wandered over Clyde's limp form. "But how?" he managed.

"The Old Magic."

"The Old Magic," repeated Demetry, sounding out the words as if they were in a foreign language.

Cendrik nodded, his face filled with glee. "Congratulations, Demetry. Your penitence is now complete. Today marks the beginning of your reformation."

Demetry looked to Cendrik with wonder, his head filled with a thousand questions. How did he perform a spell without speaking a word? Or better yet, how was he able to manifest the Old Magic now, after living his entire life without showing the slightest inkling of the gift?

"Why me? Why now?" was all Demetry was able to manage.

"In due time," replied Cendrik, smiling from ear to ear with a lopsided smirk. He lifted his heel and promptly stamped on Demetry's face.

CHAPTER
VI

THE WARDEN AND THE
WIZARD

Demetry's eyes fluttered open. As he came to, he realized that he was bobbing through the air, his body carried by a trio of guards. The gelding collar was latched tightly around Demetry's neck. Apparently the guards weren't taking any chances after what he did to Clyde. The draining effect of the Sundering Stone was palpable. Something was missing, a key part of him, his well of strength, his magic. Demetry had never felt so weak.

They were winding down a dark stairwell, traveling deeper and deeper into the earth. This was a place even Sneak had not wandered. Warden Cendrik hobbled along at the front of the procession. For the warden, every step with his lame foot was a chore, and he set a slow pace for the others to follow. Chaplain Sighelm walked beside him. The frustration was apparent in the Chaplain's face.

"If this plan of your works, how do I guarantee I get my end of the bargain?" asked Sighelm. He carried a torch, illuminating the passage with dancing light.

"You're so eager to be back in charge," said Cendrik. "It makes me wonder about your motivation."

"I'm eager to serve my gods without the crown meddling with my work."

"A noble statement, if it's true."

"It's true," snapped Sighelm. "This place ran just fine before you came along and started conducting your little experiments."

Demetry kept his body limp and motionless, deciding it would be best if the guards didn't notice he was conscious. He couldn't afford another beating. His whole body ached — the skin on his back was raw, his scalp was cut to ribbons, and his throat felt like one giant bruise. If the swelling grew much worse it would likely cut off his airway.

"I'm as eager as you are for a change in administration," said Cendrik. "But tell me, what precisely does your brotherhood intend to do with the prison, anyway?"

"That's between me and the master of my

order."

Cendrik snorted. "The master of your order serves at the pleasure of the king. As do I. As do you. Don't ever forget that."

Sighelm looked as if he might reply, but decided at the last moment to keep his opinion to himself.

Cendrik smirked. "If the prisoner does prove capable, the king will not be short on gratitude. We will all receive what we are due."

"Oh, Demetry's capable, all right. He nearly took Clyde's face clean off. There are no words for a spell like that. The Old Magic is strong in that one, I promise you."

"I couldn't agree more. But the Throne of Caper will not be satisfied with one incident. Proof takes time. You must have patience."

Sighelm spit. "I've got patience. Always have. But I also know when I'm getting the bad end of a deal. I've worked these prisoners for years trying to find the perfect subject for your pet project. I expect to be fairly compensated."

"The position of warden has always been a direct appointment of the crown. I can't guarantee anything. Still, my personal recommendation for a successor will carry weight. I promise you, I won't forget my friends."

"Waste your sweet tongue on someone else.

We're not friends, Cendrik. Just give me my due, that's all I ask. Remember, the king may approve of what you're doing here, but the Arcane Council won't. Last I heard they have the final say on admittance to the Academy Arcanum. It would be unfortunate if they got word of your experiments."

Cendrik raised his hand, stopping the procession, and slowly turned to face Sighelm. "All men get their due, Sighelm, one way or another." He placed a hand on Sighelm's cheek. The two men locked eyes. "I see everything that happens in Coljack. Always remember that. You can hide nothing from me. I can see what you have done, what you intend to do. I can see things your feeble mind hasn't yet considered. Would you like to know your future?"

"Keep your parlor tricks to yourself," said Sighelm. His body gave a slight quiver.

Cendrik grinned. "I see fire in your future. Pain. A crushing darkness. The type of death no man would envy." He gave Sighelm's cheek a soft slap and whistled merrily. "Of course, I've been wrong before." He hobbled further on down the winding stairs, calling over his shoulder. "Wake the prisoner. I'd like Demetry to see this."

One of the guards jabbed Demetry hard in the ribs. Demetry groaned in pain.

"You're back with us, eh?" Cendrik laughed. "You performed brilliantly, Demetry. Top notch. Better than I could have ever hoped. I'm proud of you."

"If you're proud of me, why don't you give me a reward? How about removing this gelding collar from my neck?" Demetry shook his head, causing the collar to rattle.

"Pride has not made me foolish," said Cendrik. "You're a dangerous young man, Demetry. A sinner, in all truth. You have embraced the Shadow and allowed the blighted spirit to enter your heart. You have used the Shadow's divine powers for your own personal gain."

"I did what you told me."

"I know you did. That is why I am so pleased." Cendrik glanced over his shoulder, grinning like a snake. "Look here, I'd like you to see this."

They had come to a narrow landing carved out of the earth. On one side of the chamber was a smooth wall of sheer cut bedrock. Hanging opposite the wall, poised high in the air was an iron-tipped battering ram. It was hoisted backward on iron chains, its colossal weight held in place by a single iron lynch pin.

"I have designed a special cell to contain men with gifts such as yours. I can't have you knocking down any more doors, you see. So you will be imprisoned far underground, and to guarantee you never escape, I've devised this fine contraption."

Demetry lifted his brow in confusion. "A battering ram? I don't understand."

"The Zeveron River lies opposite this wall," said Cendrik. He smacked the wall with the flat of his hand. It resounded with a hollow thud. "This thin layer of bedrock is all that separates us from the icy abyss. If you try to escape an alarm bell will toll, and if it does, my men are under strict orders to pull the pin on the ram. Isn't that right?"

"Yes, sir," said the guard manning the battering ram.

The gods help me, thought Demetry as he was carried past the ram. It would be hard enough sleeping underground. How could he ever find rest knowing all that separated him from certain death was a lynch pin no thicker than his thumb?

Deeper and deeper they went, so deep that the rock walls began to radiate with heat. The passage ended abruptly, the way forward blocked by a solid iron door. Demetry felt the hairs on the back of his neck stand up. There was an electricity to the air — something otherworldly and unnatural. The guards shifted uncomfortably. Sighelm clutched his cudgel tight. Even Warden Cendrik appeared ill-at-ease.

"What is this?" asked Demetry. No one answered. The guards unlocked the collar from around Demetry's neck and let his body drop to the floor. Demetry was so weak he could hardly lift himself. The rough hands of a guard forced him to stand upright.

Sighelm banged on the door with the butt end of his torch, causing cinders to rain through the air. "Walk to the door and place your hand in the holding lock."

"Is the warden out there?" called a muffled voice from the other side of the door. The voice had a southern accent. But there was something else there as well, a refinement and focus on elocution that Demetry had only heard amongst members of high society.

Sighelm and the other men eyed Warden Cendrik. For a moment it looked as if Cendrik wouldn't respond. He sighed. "Yes, I'm out here, Jeremiah."

"Where's my letter, warden? It's overdue by two weeks."

"First put your hand in the lock. Then we'll talk."

There was a long pause on the other side. A hand suddenly materialized through the wall. Demetry jumped back in fright. It took him a moment to realize there was actually a small chute cut into the rock wall that connected the corridor to the prison cell. It was barely large enough to allow an arm to pass through.

Sighelm quickly locked an iron fetter around the reaching hand. A Sundering Stone was set in the iron cuff and it immediately began to glow, illuminating the corridor in bursts of green and blue light.

Demetry's eyes narrowed. The man inside the cell was a magic, and a powerful one at that.

"The letter, warden." The hand opened expectantly.

"Not this time, Jeremiah. It will arrive soon, I'm sure."

"Then why are you here?"

Cendrik motioned to the guards, directing one to unlock the door while the other two grabbed Demetry by the shoulders. They pushed him toward the door. "Wait, what's going on?" demanded Demetry. He dragged his heels on the ground, desperate to stall.

Chaplain Sighelm stuck his hand in the air, counting down with his fingers. Three. Two. One.

The iron door was flung wide open and Demetry was tossed inside. He landed face first, collecting a mouthful of dirt. The door slammed shut behind him.

"Consider the boy your charge, a gift from the king," called Warden Cendrik, his voice now muffled by the sealed door. "What you do with the lad is completely up to you."

Demetry's new cellmate was already free from his arm shackle. He approached Demetry with lengthy strides, his movements not without menace. Demetry tried to scurry to his feet, but before he could, the man planted a foot on Demetry's chest and shoved him back to the ground.

A smokeless fire sputtered into existence in a brazier set at the center of the room, illuminating the man's face in orange light. The man possessed the dark complexion of a Kari or Donastian. Old, but not ancient, his face was pockmarked and wrinkled. A charcoal beard jutted from his chin, crafted to a careful point. "Who are you?" demanded Jeremiah.

"Demetry," he managed to squeak. The man was pressing down on Demetry's chest so hard he could hardly breathe.

"From where?"

"Taper."

"You're a magic." Jeremiah's brow furrowed. Demetry couldn't tell if that was a good or bad sign. "Before you attended Taper, were you a street rat, a beggar, a cut purse? Have you ever lived in a Yanish orphanage?" He pressed down harder with his foot, digging his toe into Demetry's sternum.

"The Nexus. I lived with my mother in the Warrens," blurted Demetry. "She died of the plague."

Jeremiah chewed his tongue, mulling over that tidbit of information. Seemingly satisfied with the answer, he stepped back and jutted out his hand, helping Demetry to his feet. "Well met, Demetry, the orphan boy from Taper. I am Jeremiah." He gave Demetry's hand a friendly shake but wouldn't let go. His eyes narrowed. "Tell me, Demetry. What part do you play in the king's ploy?"

"I don't understand." Demetry tried to pull his hand free from Jeremiah's grasp, but the man was impossibly strong. It was like having his hand stuck in a bear trap.

"Are you a spy, sent to learn my secrets?" asked Jeremiah as he slowly backed Demetry toward the wall. "Or perhaps you are an assassin, sent to kill me in my sleep?"

Demetry was quite certain he wasn't either of those things. "I'm down here because the warden thinks I'm dangerous," said Demetry. With a sharp tug he managed to yank his hand free of Jeremiah's grasp. "I used magic to break down the door of my cell. I think the warden is worried I might escape." Demetry decided it was best not to mention the fate of his last cellmate.

Jeremiah's brow furrowed. "I would prefer you don't attempt such a stunt here — you'll likely kill us both." Jeremiah snapped his fingers and the fire in the brazier flared, the flames reaching higher and higher until they licked at the ceiling. The entire space was cast in brilliant light. For the first time, Demetry realized they were standing in a massive room, even larger than the dormitory he shared with nine other boys back in Taper. The walls were rough cut granite, giving Demetry the impression that this space had been hollowed out by miners in some age long since past. The ceiling was crumbling rock and looked eager to collapse at any moment. The only thing holding the colossal weight of the earth at bay was a network of stone buttresses that crisscrossed the ceiling like a spider's web.

Jeremiah pointed to a pair of columns that flanked either side of the iron door. "The supports holding up the ceiling will give way long before the door. Try to knock down the door and this cell will become your tomb." He smacked his hands together for effect.

Demetry turned his attention to the rest of the room. To his great surprise the space actually was something quite special. There was a down mattress, a writing desk, an old rocking chair, and a pair of shelves stacked high with books. A worn rug lay in the middle of the room. A cooking pot and utensils were stacked beside the brazier. The furnishings would be considered meager in the outside world, but here, deep within the depths of Coljack, they seemed kingly indeed. Demetry couldn't help but grin. "What punishment is this?"

"It's punishment enough," replied Jeremiah with a discontented snort. "You are not free, nor will you ever be. Men are not sent to Coljack to serve their time. They are imprisoned here so that their minds turn to mush." He gave Demetry's head a soft rap with his knuckle. "Down here, beyond the reach of the sun and the evening sky, an hour can seem like a day, a day can seem like a week, and a year can be mistaken for a month. It's easy to become unhinged." There was a glint in the old man's eye — resistance was how Demetry would best describe it. Coljack had not broken him yet.

Jeremiah issued a weary sigh and sat down in his rocking chair. "We'll have to see about getting you a bed. Another chair would also be nice." Jeremiah stroked his beard. "The warden still owes me a few favors. I'll see what I can arrange."

"How long have you been down here?" asked Demetry, as he walked a circuit around the room.

Jeremiah squinted at the floor, as if the answer was somehow hidden in the stone. "Thirteen years, nine months, and three days."

Demetry's three months locked in a cell with Clyde felt like an eternity — he couldn't imagine spending thirteen years down here, buried beneath the earth, locked behind an iron door, hidden from the sun, fresh air, and trees. Pity entered his heart, then fear. *Am I destined to suffer the same fate?*

Completing his circuit, Demetry sat down cross-legged before Jeremiah. "Have you been alone all this time?"

"I have my books, my writings, my letters." Jeremiah motioned to the bookshelf. "Sometimes the warden pays me a visit. We play our games, each trying to get the other to admit more than they intend. There's a lad who thinks he's a great deal more clever than he actually is. A seer's intuition will do that."

"Warden Cendrik is a seer?" exclaimed Demetry with surprise. That might explain why Cendrik was so certain Demetry could channel the Old Magic — Cendrik had already envisioned it happening in his head. Demetry wondered what else the warden already knew.

"Indeed he is, but that's a conversation for another time," said Jeremiah, waving off the question. "Lets have a look at those wounds. It appears the Yanish Brothers were not gentle."

Demetry shuffled forward on his knees. Jeremiah prodded at the lengthy gash in Demetry's scalp. "They did a ghastly job suturing this wound. As to the bruising around your neck — it will subside in a few days, but I might be able to do something to alleviate the pain in the meantime." Jeremiah traced his finger along Demetry's wounds and muttered a few words in the ancient tongue. A blue aura emitted from his hand and Demetry's pain immediately began to ease.

It was a simple healing incantation, the type of spell even the youngest Taper acolyte knew by heart. Still, Demetry didn't know how to respond. Never in his life had a complete stranger been so kind. He watched the elderly magic work his trade in breathless wonder. Jeremiah finally reached the lacerations crisscrossing Demetry's back.

"Let me have a look." He gave Demetry's shirt a gentle tug, but the shirt didn't budge. Blood and pus had seeped from the wounds, gluing Demetry's shirt to his back.

Demetry shrugged away Jeremiah's hand.

"These scars I keep."

Jeremiah lifted an eyebrow. "You wish to bear a reminder of your torture? Do you hope the scars will give you resolve?" Jeremiah lifted the hem of his shirt, exposing a lengthy scar that ran from his hip bone to his navel. "Scars are just scars, Demetry. They don't define you. If you require them to find purpose, you are already venturing down the path of the damned."

"The lash marks stay," said Demetry sternly.

The disapproval was evident in Jeremiah's eyes, but he let the matter drop. "You look famished. How about something to eat?" He reached up the billowing sleeve of his shirt and produced an unblemished red apple.

Demetry's eyes flared wide. He collected the apple as if it were a prized possession. "They bring you food such as this?" Demetry took a greedy bite. It tasted delicious. The skin was crisp, the pulp inside was juicy and tart.

"Of course not," said Jeremiah, producing another apple from his sleeve. "You're thinking with your stomach, not your mind."

"You conjure the apple with magic."

"Correct."

"But you didn't say a word."

"Correct again."

"Which means you used the Old Magic."

Jeremiah grinned.

The realization hit Demetry like a lead weight. The cell buried in the depths of the earth. The insane security precautions. The ability to manifest the Old Magic at will. All of the evidence pointed to one conclusion. "You're not just any Jeremiah. You're Jeremiah of Brothlo, aren't you?"

Jeremiah didn't answer, but he didn't need to. The glint in the old man's eyes was answer enough. Demetry was sharing a cell with one of the most infamous magics in Laverian history. The instructors at Taper used Jeremiah's life story as a cautionary tale about the dangers of the dark arts and the treacherous allure of power. Once a promising pupil at Taper, Jeremiah abandoned his New Magic training and swore allegiance to the Wyrm. He was trained in the ways of the Old Magic by the gods themselves, and eventually became one of the most powerful magics alive.

When the War of Sundering erupted, Jeremiah became the Wyrm's top general. He slaughtered thousands in the name of his demonic gods. A villain by any measure, he should have been killed following his capture. But King Johan was unwilling to execute a man of such rare talent. Jeremiah became the king's court magic, a honed weapon used to make other men bow to the dominion of the throne. Unfortunately for the king, Jeremiah's loyalty was just a ruse. When the opportunity arose, he betrayed the king and stole his most prized possession, the Orb of Azure, an ancient artifact that contained the power to turn a mortal into a god. Given Jeremiah's current condition, he had obviously not remained free long enough to unlock the Orb's power.

"You're in here because you stole the Orb of Azure."

Jeremiah raised an eyebrow. "Do you now understand why I perceive you as a threat?"

"The king's ploy."

Jeremiah nodded. "Warden Cendrik and I have played this game for over a decade." He motioned to the furnishings and books that filled the chamber. "Cendrik bribes me with gifts, hoping they will loosen my tongue. What happened on the night the Orb of Azure disappeared, he often asks. Did I see it? Did I touch it? Did I keep it for myself? He believes his seer's intuition can pierce my shroud of misdirection and half-truths. Thus far I have thwarted his efforts. So Cendrik has brought me a new gift. You."

Demetry eyed Jeremiah with confusion. "I don't understand."

"Whether you know it or not, you have been put here to spy on me. To break me down, to win my favor, my trust, perhaps even my friendship and love. In time you will ask me of the Orb's whereabouts — your intent innocent enough. The question is, will I refuse you the answer?"

"Of course you will, just as you have done with Cendrik."

Jeremiah shrugged. "Back and forth we will go, until one day, maybe a few months from now, maybe a few years, I will finally give in. You will have all you need to buy your freedom. I have accepted a lifetime of imprisonment to keep my secret. Would you be willing to do the same?"

Demetry didn't know how to answer. If he had a way out of Coljack he would take it — wasn't that how any sensible man would behave? Despite this fact, he heard himself saying something to the contrary. "Keep your secrets concerning the Orb. Teach me your magic instead."

The proposition surprised Jeremiah. He leaned back in his chair and thumbed his chin. "I could teach you a few tricks, but in truth I am a poor instructor. I have only ever had one pupil, and I fear to say I caused more harm than good."

"Then we can learn together," said Demetry, finding himself genuinely excited by the prospect.

"You can learn to teach, and I can learn to create. I will not be a burden, I promise."

The elderly magic eyed the youth keenly. "You are dangerous, Demetry. I can sense your energy. Currently, you are wild and untamed, but there is a great potency hidden within you. Magic is treacherous, and the type that I know is most treacherous of all. If you are to become my pupil you must promise me this; you are not to press me for knowledge until I say you are ready. A true student must bow to the teacher's will."

"You have my promise," said Demetry. He crossed his hands over his heart and edged closer.

Jeremiah chewed at his lip, still unsure. Finally, he sighed with resignation. "Very well," said Jeremiah, his frown slowly turning into a smile. "Lesson one is the apple." He held up an apple and began his lecture.

CHAPTER VII

MASTER AND APPRENTICE

T he essential rule that you must understand, before I can teach you another thing, is that all you ever learned at Taper was a lie." Jeremiah was standing behind his desk, using it as a lectern. Scribbled notes and crossed out lists covered the surface. "That knowledge served as a distraction to deny you your full potential."

"Truly, you are exaggerating," said Demetry. He was lounging on the bumpy hay-filled mattress the warden called a bed.

Jeremiah gave him a look that implied he most definitely was not. "Do this, create an apple for me."

Demetry sat up cross-legged and began to murmur the words to the spell. It was one of the hundreds of New Magic spells Jeremiah had taught him in the past few months. Demetry was eager to learn the Old Magic, but for some reason Jeremiah was holding back. To prove he was ready, Demetry worked on each New Magic incantation until he had it practiced to perfection. Then he would practice some more, often staying awake long after Jeremiah had fallen asleep. Demetry hoped his hard work ethic would convince Jeremiah he was ready to take the next step. Thus far, it had not. Demetry was beginning to worry Jeremiah was going to back out on his promise.

"*He's holding back because he fears you,*" whispered a nagging voice in the recesses of Demetry's mind. "*He knows what you are. He knows what you will become. Jeremiah's no better than the headmaster and his brat nephew.*"

Demetry silenced the paranoid opinion with a shake of his head and focused on the task at hand. His voice rose and fell as he began the New Magic incantation to summon an apple. The words painted an image in his mind; red flesh, spongy interior, seeds black as jet. He could feel the fruit start to take form in his hand. Only one more cycle through the refrain and it would materialize. Suddenly, something thwacked him in the head. Demetry looked up to discover Jeremiah had his arm cocked back and was ready to throw a second apple.

"What was that?" demanded Demetry, raising his hands in defense.

"An apple."

"I don't understand."

"Life is an endless game of twisting words to match your thoughts. Yet which is the weaker lot?" Jeremiah edged closer, tossing the apple from hand to hand. His lips were curled in a devilish smirk. "Words obscure our true meaning. Thoughts are endless. Thus the New Magic limits us. Do you know who taught men how to use the New Magic?"

"The Guardians."

Jeremiah nodded.

"When the first generation of magic wielders came into their powers, there were no spells, no incantations, no knowledge of the void, or comprehension of the Sundered Soul," said Jeremiah, his voice deepening as he took on the tone he often used while lecturing. "The first generation knew only one type of magic — the Old Magic, the magic of the mind. The results were catastrophic. Cities burned, warlocks claimed dominion, entire empires fell."

"The Fall of Eremor."

Jeremiah nodded again. "The Guardians provided a solution. They taught the survivors a diluted form of magic to prevent such disasters from occurring in the future. The New Magic served its purpose, but it left men ill prepared to combat the demi-gods when they turned against the mortal races."

"Is that why the Wyrm taught you the Old Magic?"

Jeremiah laughed. "The Wyrm taught me the Old Magic because they wanted a weapon. They used me, just like King Johan did. Just like you are doing right now."

Demetry scoffed at the notion. "I'm not using you."

"Are you certain of that?"

"I seek knowledge, Jeremiah, nothing more," said Demetry, mostly believing it to be the truth. "I have read the forbidden text of the *Paserani Haote*. I know that the mortal mind is far stronger than my instructors at Taper would have me believe. I want to unlock my potential. I'm ready."

Jeremiah sighed. "You think you are ready, but you are not. You never will be. Still, I can't delay forever."

"Then you will teach me?"

Jeremiah smirked. "Do you know the words of a spell that would turn stone into life?" Inexplicably, moss sprung from the walls, grass grew from the floor, and all about them was green.

Aghast, Demetry scrambled to the edge of his bed, watching in wonder as life abounded within the dank subterranean cell.

"There are no words for such a spell, but that does not mean it cannot be done," said Jeremiah. "The words of a New Magic spell serve only as a medium through which to channel your focus. They cripple you, denying you your inherent strength. The Old Magic, on the other hand, is limited only by the power of your mind."

Demetry grabbed the leaves of a nearby plant that had miraculously taken root on the face of the rock wall. It was the first green thing he had seen in nearly a year. He immediately recoiled as a thousand pinpricks trailed down the length of his finger. It felt as if his hand was on fire.

He sucked at his fingers but it did nothing to alleviate the pain. If anything, the burning sensation was spreading, traveling up his wrist and forearm. The plants continued to grow, encroaching on his bed with reaching limbs and twisting vines that sprouted jagged thorns. A milky substance seeped from their leaves. It fell like teardrops, hissing and popping as it splattered on his mattress.

Demetry shied away from the plants. "I understand your point, Jeremiah. You can stop now."

"Do you truly?" Jeremiah walked through the tangled bramble, the leaves and branches parting before him. "There is no tool in the world more powerful than the mind. But the mind can be frightful at times, full of irrational thoughts, hatred, fear, inner anguish. There is a reason why the Guardians tried to prevent mortals from using the Old Magic. We don't have the discipline to wield it properly. A good intention can be twisted by the slightest dark thought. And a bad intention..." Jeremiah let the words linger.

Flowers sprouted from the branches, their bulbs the color of blood. Demetry swore the petals had teeth. The pistils of the flowers wiggled like tongues.

"Will you use such powers for good? For evil? Will you use it to escape the confines of this cell?"

Demetry batted away the flowers as they drew near. "I will use the Old Magic as you instruct me." His hands burned from the poison dripping from the petals.

"Ah, I see. You will surrender your free will to an old dotard."

Demetry huddled at the center of his bed, the only place free of the stinging flowers. "What do you want me to say?"

"Words will not suffice. I need you to understand." He tapped Demetry between the eyes. "You are about to venture down a most perilous path. You must be prepared, lest your mind grow perverted and the Shadow take you." Jeremiah snapped his fingers and the poisonous bramble turned to vapor. He turned his back and walked away. "Spend the rest of the day thinking about what I said. We will begin with the Old Magic tomorrow."

Demetry peeked over the side of his bed. There was no physical sign that the plants had ever existed. He examined his hands. The burn marks were gone. Had it all been an illusion, a trick on his mind? Only Jeremiah knew the answer.

• • •

Demetry awoke the next morning to once again discover Jeremiah standing behind his desk. The clutter of notes had been cleared away. In their place lay three objects set in a row. Each one was covered by a piece of cloth.

"Today you will learn the most basic principle of the Old Magic." Jeremiah's deep and sonorous voice echoed in the chamber. "But first, I would like you to demonstrate your capabilities with the New Magic."

Demetry rose groggily from bed and walked over to the table. "What would you like me to do?" asked Demetry, as he rubbed the sleep from his eyes.

"I would like you to transfer these three objects to that bench." Jeremiah had set the bench from the table near the door to their cell. "We'll start with an easy one." Jeremiah lifted the first piece of cloth, revealing a fist-sized rock.

Demetry bent over and examined the rock. There was nothing special about it. Jeremiah had likely chipped the rock from the earthen wall of their cell.

"How would you move this rock using the New Magic they taught you at Taper?"

"Magnetism," announced Demetry, glad to actually know the answer to one of Jeremiah's questions for once. Demetry used to practice manipulating metallic objects by retrieving lost fishhooks from a pond near his former dormitory. In truth, it wasn't a very difficult skill to master. Even Joshua, novice as he was, was capable of levitating rocks that contained only trace amounts of iron ore.

"Ah, but which spell will you use?"

Demetry knew a few dozen off the top of his head, but finding the right spell would take a bit of consideration. It all depended on the object he was trying to move. The object's weight was one factor, the ratio of magnetic to non-magnetic materials was another. Settling on a spell, Demetry spun his arms in the air and chanted a few words in the ancient tongue. *"Mati muttí hajute ise habrat op iat."*

The stone rose into the air and slowly floated over the expanse. During the transit, the stone wobbled a bit more on its axis than Demetry would have liked, but it was an otherwise successful casting. The stone settled atop the far bench with a gentle clack. Demetry grinned, feeling rather pleased with himself.

Jeremiah looked unimpressed. "Wipe that stupid smirk off your face — you did nothing to be proud of. You picked the wrong spell, and you nearly lost control of the stone midway through the flight. Now focus — it only gets harder from here." He lifted the next piece of fabric, revealing a clay jar filled to the brim with water. "Move the water. Leave the jar."

Demetry could utilize the New Magic to freeze the water solid or boil it down to nothing, but he didn't have an idea how to make the water float through the air. He was about to admit he was stumped when a thought entered his head.

Demetry collected the stone from the far bench

and dropped it into the jar.

Jeremiah raised his eyebrow curiously.

"*Lisí ijei oprot lae,*" said Demetry. The water instantaneously froze solid, causing the jar to split down the middle and topple over. What remained was a jar shaped ice sculpture with a stone entombed in its base.

Making a few adjustments to the magnetic levitation spell he had used a few moments earlier, Demetry once again seized the stone with his magic, only this time the stone carried the ice sculpture with it. He drew the levitating ice sculpture to a halt directly above the bench.

"*Lisí lae oprot ijei.*" The ice melted, sending a cascade of liquid water raining down on the bench. As proud as he was of the feat, Demetry knew better than to smile this time.

"Very clever, I'll give you that," said Jeremiah. "But it involved far too many steps and wasted too much time." Jeremiah waved his hand in the air, and the spilled water immediately boiled down to nothing, leaving behind no trace that it was ever there.

"I know how to boil water," said Demetry, feeling a bit annoyed.

"I would hope so," replied Jeremiah. "That's one of the first spells an acolyte learns at Taper.

But what you fail to comprehend is that the water isn't gone — it has simply changed states. Because we can see, touch, and taste water in its liquid and solid states, we innately understand its properties. Liquid water flows, it takes on the shape of its container, and it wants always to equalize. Water expands when it freezes, granting it the strength to shatter solid objects. But what are the properties of water vapor?"

Demetry shrugged. "Water, be it in its liquid or solid state, has substance and weight. It can be manipulated to the magic wielder's advantage. Turning water into vapor wastes its potential. It's simply gone." Demetry waved his hand through the air, as if that might prove his point.

"Wrong again." Jeremiah snapped his fingers, and a ball of water suddenly materialized in the air above the broken jar. It hovered there for a split second before it splashed down, drenching the table and floor.

"I see no lost potential there," said Jeremiah, smirking from ear to ear. He threw Demetry the piece of cloth and motioned for him to clean up the mess. Demetry begrudgingly went to work mopping the table and floor with the cloth.

"The Old Magic grants me the ability to manipulate the elements in a manner the New

Magic simply cannot," said Jeremiah, continuing on with his lecture. "I am not limited by the spells I have mastered or the elements of nature I can see. Remember that for this last test." Jeremiah sidestepped to the last hidden object on the table and lifted the cloth.

Demetry didn't even bother to rise from his work cleaning up the spilled water — there was no point. He knew he couldn't do what Jeremiah was asking. The last object was a feather. Without a doubt, it was the lightest object in the room, yet Demetry hadn't the slightest idea how to move it with the New Magic. "Would you like me to disintegrate the feather and reconstitute it on the other side of the room?" asked Demetry, feeling a bit frustrated.

"Oh, this one is easy." Jeremiah blew softly, and the feather fluttered off the table, twirling on the stream of air Jeremiah had created with his mouth.

"Very funny," said Demetry. He gave up trying to clean the spilled water and threw the cloth on the table. "I could have done that."

"But can you do this?" The feather went shooting through the air as fast as a dart projected from a blowgun. It embedded itself into the far wall.

Demetry was aghast.

"You lived in the Nexus, yes? Then surely you have witnessed the great whirlwinds that tear across the Soccoto Plains during spring. You claim that air has no substance, but in truth you know better. Air has enough substance to wear down mountains, to scour valleys, to create waves in the ocean. Air also has the power to turn the most innocuous objects into something as deadly as an arrow launched from a bow."

Demetry's eyes wandered from the table to the wall and back again as he tried to figure out how Jeremiah had performed the task. "How?" was all he could manage.

"The Old Magic manipulates objects at their most minuscule level. Do you wish to levitate a feather? Draw it forward by creating a void in the air. Do you wish to turn liquid water into vapor? Excite its individual particles until it transforms into gas. But don't ignore the perils involved."

The large brazier set in the middle of the room suddenly flared to life, its flames licking high in the air. "I would like you to compare the fire in this brazier to a campfire in a dry forest," instructed Jeremiah. "Within the brazier, the fire is contained, controlled, safe. That is the essence of a New Magic spell. Now consider the campfire. A single stray ember might ignite the entire forest."

Jeremiah walked forward and stuck his finger to the middle of Demetry's forehead. "That stray ember is your mind. Let it wander, and the consequences can be grave."

Jeremiah motioned toward the remnants of the puddle surrounding the bench. The water began to bubble and steam, boiling away to nothing in a matter of seconds. But even after the last drop had vanished, Demetry still detected a soft hiss. He looked to Jeremiah, confused.

"Using the Old Magic for something as simple as boiling water comes with its own perils. Nearly everything contains water. The soil, trees, bricks, even that bench. A momentary lapse in focus can prove catastrophic." Suddenly, there was a terrible hiss, like a wet log outgassing in a fire, then the bench exploded apart. Shards of wood were sent flying every which way.

"The gods help me," cried Demetry as he leapt halfway across the room.

Jeremiah didn't so much as flinch. "Are you beginning to understand the dangers of the Old Magic?"

Demetry was starting to piece together some of the darker implications of Jeremiah's lesson. Blood was mostly water, or so Demetry's alchemy instructor at Taper had told him. "If you can do that to a bench what might you do to a man?"

Jeremiah didn't respond — the answer was obvious. He turned toward Demetry, all humor gone from his face. "The Old Magic exists within the world of the miniature — particles so infinitely small you could not see them with the strongest looking glass. Tempting, isn't it, to know that you could manipulate the most basic elements of our physical world."

Demetry chewed at his lip. The New Magic was slow and tedious, but extremely precise. Accidental outcomes were rare. With the New Magic, he wasn't at risk of inadvertently killing another man while boiling a kettle of tea. "Is such power worth the risk?" wondered Demetry aloud.

"That is the wizard's dilemma, isn't it?" said Jeremiah. "To practice self-restraint and walk blissfully ignorant in the light, or to embrace one's true potential and enter the dark dominion of the damned. A man might lose his soul in such an endeavor."

"Or a man might become akin to the gods."

Jeremiah nodded. "When your training is complete you will have mastery of the physical world. Earth, wind, water, and fire will be yours to command. Are you ready to begin?"

"Yes," said Demetry breathlessly.

"Good." Jeremiah plucked the feather from the wall and held it aloft between his forefinger and thumb. "Now, make this feather fly."

CHAPTER
VIII

LETTERS AND SECRETS

As Demetry practiced the Old Magic, one thing soon became apparent — Jeremiah had not overstated the dangers. The Old Magic was fickle, and glorious, and devastating, and beautiful all at once. On days when Demetry's mind was clear, he felt like his powers were boundless. On days when his mind was clouded, it seemed as if nothing went right.

Once, while practicing his pyromancy, he set a pot of water on fire, as impossible as that might seem. He would have probably suffocated from smoke inhalation had Jeremiah not quickly intervened by throwing a lid over the fire. Another time Demetry lost his focus and accidentally conjured a miniature thunderstorm located entirely within the confines of their cell. Jeremiah had to scramble to keep his notes and books from being ruined, all the while dodging bolts of lightning. Demetry's ears rang for days thereafter.

Demetry's greatest problem was his concentration. The New Magic used words and hand motions to lull the mind into a meditative state. Because of this, it was all but guaranteed that the spell Demetry conjured was in line with his original intentions.

The Old Magic was not so forgiving. A momentary collapse in concentration could produce an unintended consequence, or worse still, cause the spell to come undone with catastrophic results. Demetry only had to consider Joshua's fate to understand the risks he was taking. Joshua had misspoken one word and the consequence was fatal. What would be the result of one ill-timed thought with the Old Magic?

Jeremiah did his best to keep Demetry safe. Since Old Magic spells had no words, much of Jeremiah's instruction was focused on four core techniques: clearing the mind of distracting thoughts, envisioning the intended outcome, channeling the Sundered Soul, and releasing hold of the enchantment upon completion. Because a failure to complete any one step could have catastrophic results, Jeremiah approached Demetry's training with the sternness of a drill master. This was not surprising, given his history as a Wyrm general. Jeremiah led vast legions of dark children during the War of Sundering — training a young lad in the ways of the Old Magic was no challenge in comparison.

The only thing that ever disrupted Demetry's daily routine was the occasional visit by Warden Cendrik. Every few weeks the warden would descend the endless flight of stairs with a bottle of wine in hand. On such occasions, Demetry would sulk to the corner of the room and keep to himself. He was not about to forget the abuse he had received from Cendrik's men.

Demetry's dislike of Cendrik didn't stop Jeremiah from conversing with the warden like they were old chums. The two would often lounge for hours beside the glowing brazier talking quietly about history and the Sundered Gods. Sometimes Cendrik would challenge Jeremiah to a game of bones. The two men would sit hunched over on either side of the board like venerable generals, Cendrik with his cane draped across his lap, and Jeremiah squinting at the board to focus his aging eyes. They would play for hours without saying a word, moving their pieces and rolling the die with practiced precision. Jeremiah won more often than not, which didn't seem to bother Cendrik in the slightest. Cendrik claimed it was the only time he ever got to play a fair game. His seer's intuition typically enabled him to read his opponent's next move, but not so with Jeremiah. Jeremiah's mind was like a dark cave.

Demetry guessed at Warden Cendrik's true intention — he was attempting to spy on Demetry's mind. Demetry could often feel the probing touch of Cendrik's third eye. Was he checking on Demetry's progress? Was he searching for the whereabouts of the Orb? Demetry could not say. All he knew was that another set of eyes in his head was not welcome — the space was already far too crowded.

On his way out the door, Cendrik would often hand Jeremiah a letter. As soon as they could hear the telltale *thunk, tap, thunk,* of Cendrik ascending the stairwell, Jeremiah would retire to his desk and break the seal on the letter. He would spend the rest of the evening hunched over examining the letter with rapt interest. He would set into the parchment with a pen, underlining words, circling letters, and jotting down a cipher in the margins. It didn't take long for Demetry to figure out these were no ordinary letters — someone was feeding Jeremiah secrets from the outside world. Sometimes Jeremiah would laugh, at other times

Demetry could detect a hint of moisture in the old man's eyes. Whoever the letters were from, they were bittersweet, that was for certain. Jeremiah never let Demetry read a single one of the letters — he would always burn them immediately after he was finished. When asked about the letters, Jeremiah would change the subject, and when that didn't work he would grow hostile.

"A boy ought to know when to keep his nose out of someone else's affairs."

Demetry could only shrug and add this mystery to the lengthy list of unknowns he already had concerning the old man.

The anniversary of Demetry's imprisonment came and went. Demetry stopped bothering to gauge the passage of time. He focused on his training every waking hour, sleeping only when he was too tired to move. Jeremiah often had to remind him to eat. Demetry would do so grudgingly — there was always more to do, more to practice, more skills to hone.

Jeremiah watched Demetry's progress with a mixture of pride and worry. Demetry was growing restless, and he was having a hard time hiding it. He began to see the cavern, which at first seemed like a grand space filled with fine furnishings, for what it really was — his tomb. He wanted to try his powers in the real world, to show his strength to those who condemned him to the depths of Coljack. But he had promised Jeremiah he would not attempt to escape. Even so, the thought was always there, gnawing at the back of his mind like a cancer.

"You did nothing wrong. You deserve to be free," the voice in his head would whisper when Demetry was feeling especially disheartened. *"Cages contain the weak. You are strong. You are powerful. You must break free."*

On most days, Demetry woke before Jeremiah so that he could get a few minutes of practice in before Jeremiah began his daily lessons. One morning Demetry was practicing levitating books — a feat made all the more difficult by the distracting sound of his mentor's incessant snoring — when a roll of parchment came shooting through the locking portal beside the cell door. It landed on the floor with a hollow thud. The sudden commotion broke Demetry's concentration, and the collection of books he was practicing with came crashing to the ground.

He winced, half expecting a firm scolding from Jeremiah, but the old man remained silent. Demetry was pleased to discover Jeremiah had somehow managed to sleep through the ruckus.

He quickly returned the books to their shelf. "Wake up, Jeremiah. You have a letter," called Demetry, once everything was back in order. Jeremiah did not reply. If anything, his snoring grew louder.

Demetry gave Jeremiah's shoulder a gentle shake. "You have a letter." Jeremiah muttered something unintelligible, and then rolled over and continued to snore.

Demetry's eyes wandered back to the piece of rolled parchment lying by the door. It was sealed shut with a red wax stamp.

"*Don't you want to know who it's from?*" Demetry scowled. Joshua's voice always seemed to creep into his consciousness whenever his advice was least welcome.

Demetry collected the letter from the floor. The wax seal bore two symbols — an eagle and a rising sun. This was the seal of some great house, no doubt, but Demetry couldn't remember which one. He cursed himself for not paying more attention to such matters in school.

"*Break the seal. Read the letter,*" whispered the nagging voice. "*How can you trust Jeremiah without knowing who these letters are from? Maybe he and Cendrik are playing you. The two seem chummy enough. Perhaps their games of bones are just a ruse. Their true communications come through the letters."*

Demetry grunted with frustration. Why couldn't he trust anyone?

He slid his finger along the crease in the parchment and broke the seal. Demetry felt guilty the moment he did it, but there was no going back. His eyes quickly darted across the page, catching snippets of the letter's contents until he came to the end.

Yours Always, Calycia.

Demetry had only a second to wonder about the name. The letter suddenly flew from his hands, whipping from his grasp so quickly it cut grooves into his finger tips. Jeremiah snatched the letter out of the air.

"Mind your own matters," snapped Jeremiah, rising from his bed. "You know full well this letter was meant for me. I…"

Demetry raised his hand. "You might want to hold your scolding for later," said Demetry. He was beginning to piece together some of the words he had caught while scanning the letter — none of the news sounded good. "The letter brings dark tidings."

Jeremiah scowled. He hurried over to his desk and pulled the brazier close, illuminating his face with orange light. He unrolled the parchment, setting a small stone on each corner to keep it flat. His eyes quickly wandered over the text. For once his pen was idle — he didn't bother to jot down a single note in the margin. A look of deep concern creased his face when he reached the end.

"There is plague in the Nexus and parties of dragoon raiders south of the wall," said Demetry, reciting what he had gleaned from the letter before it was snatched away.

With a heavy sigh, Jeremiah let the parchment roll shut. "What you say is correct. But there is more hidden by the cipher. The plague is running through the cities like wildfire, killing most who show symptoms. People are fleeing the cities in droves, spreading the plague further afield. The king speaks of quarantine, and all this while the main host of the dark enemy is amassing north of the wall. War is coming. The plague is just a precursor, meant to sow chaos and weaken our defenses."

"Our defenses?" Demetry's eyes narrowed. "That is spoken like a man who still serves the king."

"I serve no one but myself," said Jeremiah, his voice taking on a dangerous tone. "Still, there are some matters where the king and I share a common enemy. Dragoons are friend to no man."

Of the three races of dark children, dragoons were largely considered to be the most dangerous. Bred by the Wyrm to be duplicitous and deadly creatures, dragoons had more in common with crocodiles than they did with the race of men. Demetry always found it amazing that Jeremiah had somehow managed to control vast legions of the beasts during the War of Sundering.

"What threat could the dragoons truly pose?" asked Demetry. "I thought they were slaughtered nearly to extinction during the War of Sundering."

"If only that were true," said Jeremiah. "Thousands of dark children managed to flee into the wastes of Eremor. If they've been breeding and multiplying all this time, their numbers could be great, enough for an invasion."

Demetry snorted. "Let them come. It would be fair justice for the king to meet his demise at the sharp end of a dragoon's talon." He tried to peek over Jeremiah's shoulder and get a second look at the letter.

"Don't say such things," said Jeremiah. He waved his hand, shooing Demetry aside.

"You were the general who once marshaled dragoons into battle, not me," snapped Demetry, growing frustrated by Jeremiah's hypocrisy.

"Aye? Well I regret that choice. My biggest

mistake was not seeing the Wyrm for what they were from the start. I have lived the rest of my life struggling for penance."

"Its easy to speak of regrets, yet why did you serve the Wyrm in the first place?"

"May you never be so tempted," said Jeremiah with a solemn shake of his head. "The Wyrm promised me knowledge and power beyond compare. In my youthful ignorance I could not say no. Would you have acted any differently?"

Probably not, Demetry had to admit. He had taken the *Paserani Haote* from the headmaster's study, drawn by the allure of hidden knowledge. If the gods of old had offered Demetry unbridled power, he probably wouldn't have hesitated.

Jeremiah placed the letter atop the glowing coals of the brazier. The parchment curled in on itself like a dying spider. Demetry caught the signature at the bottom one last time before it vanished into flames.

"This Calycia, who is she?" asked Demetry, growing bold.

Jeremiah seemed reluctant to answer. He sat in silence as the letter was slowly reduced to white ash. "She is someone I had no right to love," he said finally, his voice hardly a whisper. "Someone who made the mistake of loving me in return. We have both paid dearly for our indiscretions."

"Why does the warden allow you to receive the letters?"

"As far as I know, he has no say in the matter. The king is the one who ordered the letters to be delivered. It's his way of reminding me of the stakes. After all these years he still has ways to hurt me."

"He could have her killed."

Jeremiah nodded.

"Yet the king refrains. Why?"

"The king still believes he can wrestle the whereabouts of the Orb from my head. If he kills her, he would have nothing left to use against me. He would be a snake without venom."

"And this Calycia is the reason you haven't tried to escape?"

Jeremiah raised an eyebrow at that. "Need I remind you of the nature of this cell. A thousand tons of rock hang overhead. As powerful as I might seem, I cannot hold the weight of a mountain upon my back."

"What if I could open the door?"

"Say you could. The alarm bells would toll and the floodgate would open. You and I would drown before we made it halfway up the stairs. Or have you devised a spell to sprout gills?"

"Anything is possible with the Old Magic," said Demetry, his voice dripping with sarcasm.

Jeremiah's whole body shook with frustration. "I'm teaching you the Old Magic so that you can find purpose in your confinement," snapped Jeremiah, "not so you can daydream about ways to get yourself killed. Stop being so foolish!"

Demetry stared at his feet. He had never seen Jeremiah so angry.

"Besides, maybe I deserve this," said Jeremiah, taking on a softer tone.

"You don't believe that."

"Don't I? I served the Wyrm, Demetry. I killed countless, burned cities, led legions of dark children. Have you ever seen what a squadron of dragoons can do to a host of unarmed villagers? I have, because I was the one giving the orders. My sins are too numerous to count. Perhaps a dank hole in the bottom of the earth is precisely where I deserve to spend my final days."

"What about me? I'm young. I have decades of life ahead of me. Would you condemn me to this same fate? One day you will die, and I will sit here in this cell suffocating in the darkness for the rest of my life."

"You know of my crime, what about yours?" said Jeremiah. He looked all too similar to the instructors at Taper, his eyes glinting with self-righteousness. "I'm no fool Demetry. Innocent men don't end up at Coljack. What did you do?"

It was the first time in all these months that Jeremiah ever asked the questions.

"N-n-nothing," stuttered Demetry, quailing beneath Jeremiah's stern gaze. "It was a mistake. A misunderstanding."

"How many men did you kill?"

"None." The scars in Demetry's back began to throb.

"What forbidden spell did you perform?"

Demetry shook his head, refusing to answer. "What I did, I did out of love," he finally whispered.

Jeremiah sneered. "We all find ways to justify our dark deeds, Demetry. Forgiveness comes to those who accept their own failings and direct the blame where it truly belongs." He turned his back on Demetry and returned to his desk. "I will hear no more talk of escape. You made me a promise when you began your training. I expect you to keep it. A man is only as good as his word."

Demetry bristled with rage, but held his tongue. How could Jeremiah be so blind to the injustice staring him in the face? This cell, this prison, this sentence — none of it was fair.

There was no justice in this world, Demetry surmised, only men, and the kings that lorded over them like gods. Jeremiah might be willing to accept his place in the world. Demetry was not.

CHAPTER
IX

PLAGUE AND WAR

Demetry knew he was dreaming when he saw his mother's face. Her cheeks and forehead were covered with scabs. Her hair, which she typically kept braided and raised in a bun, was a disheveled mess. Her eyes were pale and rheumy, lifeless. No breath passed her lips.

Demetry tried to feed her anyway, smashing up a bundle of carrots he had stolen from a market vendor until they formed a thin paste. It was what his mother would have done if he was sick. He tried to force a spoonful of the orange paste into her mouth, but her teeth wouldn't part. She'd been like that for over a day, and Demetry didn't know what to do.

When his mother first took ill, he ran to his neighbors begging for help. No one would even open their door. They all barked instructions from

171

behind closed doors, their voices muffled by the thin wooden planks they hoped would protect them from the plague. *"Keep her warm,"* they advised. *"Place a damp cloth on her forehead to ease the fever. Make sure she drinks plenty of water. Pray."*

Praying was never a problem for Demetry. Like most who lived in the Warrens, his mother was a pious woman. She made certain Demetry had the entire pantheon of gods memorized before he was old enough to form coherent sentences. By the time Demetry was four years of age, he could recite several dozen prayers by heart.

He prayed to Vacia first. She was the patron goddess of the sick, and thus, the most likely to come to his mother's aid. When that didn't work, he tried the Weaver. She was responsible for orchestrating the fates of mankind. Surely matters of life and death fell under the goddess's purview. When his mother's fever didn't break, he grew fearful that he might have offended one of the other deities. The god-saint Yansarian was the most likely culprit. It was well-known that Yansarian was a fickle god and prone to wrath when ignored. To make up for his ignorance, Demetry recited ten Divine Blessings, and then proceeded to flagellate himself with a whip he fashioned out of horse-leather. Once again, his prayers went unanswered.

If anything, his mother's condition was worsening.

Demetry made several trips in search of fresh water, but each time he ventured from home he found guards stationed at the community well. "The wells are poisoned," Demetry heard one woman say. "The gods are punishing us for our sins," lamented another. During his final trip to the well, he discovered that the guards had vacated their post. They were no longer needed — the well was entombed in a fresh layer of bricks and mortar.

Sheets and blankets they had aplenty, but his mother kept soiling the bed. By the end of the third night the only remaining clean linen was a threadbare sheet that was only suitable for the summer months. His mother's teeth were constantly chattering, and her body would go through fits of uncontrollable tremors. Demetry tried using his own body heat to keep her warm, but she kept shoving him away, muttering in a barely comprehensible voice that she didn't want to make him sick. When she finally stopped shivering on the sixth day, even Demetry, though just a child, knew it was a bad sign. Her body had run through its reserves. She teetered now on that fragile line between life and death.

He spent the rest of the night praying for divine intervention. His youthful mind could only wonder why the gods continued to ignore his pleas. Had he recited the prayers improperly? Had he asked the wrong gods for help? Perhaps he was too tarnished by sin to deserve aid — he had stolen the carrots from a merchant, after all. He fell asleep first cursing the gods, and then begging for their forgiveness.

He awoke the next morning to a ruckus in the alley. Women were crying, children were screaming. The last time that happened a mob came rushing through the Warrens breaking down doors and looting houses. Demetry was horrified. He grabbed his mother's stiff arm and pulled it around his body, nestling into the hollow between her arms and legs.

There were more voices in the alley; this time it was the deep-throated growl of men. The handle to the door rattled as someone checked to see if it was locked.

"Is anyone alive in there?" The man beat at the door with the flat of his fist.

Demetry considered begging the gods for help, but decided they were likely still mad at him from the previous night. Instead, he hid his eyes against his mother's chest and hoped the men in the alley would just go away.

"Hand me the axe."

The heavy thwack of metal striking wood filled the air. The door rattled on its hinges until it finally gave way, swinging inward in a hail of splinters and shattered planking.

A hulking figure stepped inside with an axe dangling in his hand. His clothes were filthy, stained with nightsoil, blood, and the gods knew what else. A handkerchief covered his mouth and nose.

"Fetch the cart. There are two more in here," said the man, calling over his shoulder.

"The cart can wait," replied a voice from outside. A second man shouldered his way into the room. He was similarly dressed as the first, but his frame was thin to the point of being emaciated, and his face was narrow and sharp like a rat. "Fill your pockets before the magistrate comes to investigate." The thin man's pockets were already so full they looked ripe to burst. He began to rummage through the drawers, pocketing anything he found of value — a coin purse, his mother's favorite ring, a glass perfume bottle, a tarnished spoon.

"Fine, don't help me," said the hulking man, shaking his head with disapproval. With a weary sigh, the hulking man went to work. He grabbed Demetry's mother by the leg and began to drag her toward the door. This left Demetry lying all alone on the floor.

Demetry's stomach turned over in a panic. He jumped to his feet and latched onto his mother's legs. "Leave her alone!" he screamed at the top of his lungs.

The hulking man's eyes flared with dismay. He dropped Demetry's mother and backed away, pulling his handkerchief tight about his face. "The gods help me, we've got a live one here!"

The thin man dropped a kettle he was eyeing and spun on his heels. He gave Demetry a once-over with his eyes. "You sick, boy? Are you feeling hot or achy? Have you got a case of the shits?"

Demetry shook his head.

"Could be he's not sick," suggested the hulking man, still clutching the handkerchief tight to ward off the ill humors in the air.

"Could be," agreed the thin man. He cautiously took a knee beside Demetry. He turned Demetry's face from side to side and then lifted Demetry's shirt to check his belly and back. Demetry felt like a pig being inspected for sale at a market. "Not a boil or pockmark on the lad's body," the man finally reported. There was a noticeable hint of relief in his voice.

"Check again," said the hulking man. He had

backed himself all the way to the far side of the room.

The thin man gave the hulking man a dismissive wave. "Look at the boy's mother. She's been dead for awhile. If the boy was going to take sick it would have already happened. He's clean."

A flicker of interest suddenly showed in the hulking man's eyes. "Do you think he bears the Creator's blessing?"

The thin man chewed at his tongue. "They pulled a babe out of the east ward last week. Whole family was dead, save the boy. The Arcane Council figures he's a magic. Supposedly, there's something about his latent powers that makes him immune to the sickness."

"What do we do with him?"

The thin man looked over his shoulder, making certain no one was standing at the door eavesdropping on their conversation. Satisfied they were alone, he collected a soiled blanket from the corner of the room. "How about we wrap the lad up in one of these blankets and cart him out of here before the magistrate gets wise. The Yanish Brotherhood will pay good silver for a boy like this."

The hulking man's face turned sour. "That they will. But do you have any idea what the brotherhood will do with the boy?"

"Do you think I give a damn about the brotherhood's indiscretions? This lad could pay my rent for half the year. Now quick, help me wrap him up." The thin man grabbed Demetry by the shoulder, but just then, there came a knock on the door.

All eyes turned to discover a black-cloaked figure with the beaked face of a bird standing in the threshold.

The hulking man gulped audibly.

The thin man was more clever with his response. "My lord, the gods have blessed us," said the thin man, bowing with the grace of a Divine Supplicant. "We have discovered a young boy untouched by the plague." He draped the blanket over Demetry's shoulders in a fatherly fashion.

Demetry said nothing, he was stunned to petrified silence by the sudden appearance of the bird-faced man. He was certain the man was one of the winged gods of Calaban, come to punish Demetry for his deviant ways. What was left of the stolen bundle of carrots lay on the floor by the door.

"A lucky find," said the bird-faced man. His voice came out muffled and harsh through his beaked mouth. His black, unblinking eyes were locked squarely on Demetry. Demetry began to tremble.

The bird-faced man stepped through the threshold, passing the stolen carrots without giving them a glance. He reached up to his face and unfastened a hidden clasp. His face came off in his hands — a mask, Demetry realized with a sudden sense of relief. The man's true face was plain, albeit kind. A grin parted the man's lips as he took a knee before Demetry.

Demetry wrinkled his nose at the man's strong scent. The man wore a sachet stuffed with garlic bulbs. Demetry reached for the silken bag, and the man graciously let him play with it.

"Do you have a father, boy?" asked the lord.

Demetry had to think about the question for a moment. There were men who came and went. Some of them even called Demetry son, but his mother had never let him call any of the men father. He decided no was the correct answer and shook his head.

The lord didn't appear surprised. "Magics lust after women just like any other man. This wouldn't be the first time a whore reared a child with the Blessing." He stood upright, a grin of satisfaction on his face. "The boy is the correct age and appears unusually hale given the circumstances. I'd say he's a perfect candidate."

"I was thinking the same thing," said the thin man. He kept his eyes averted toward the floor.

"Of course you did," said the lord, grinning, always grinning. He patted Demetry on the head. "The boy reeks of death. I want him stripped down and given a good scrubbing. Get him new clothes and deliver him to the Arcane Council.

"That will, ah, have costs, my lord."

The magistrate reached into a hidden pocket in his cloak and produced a silver coin. He flipped it to the thin man. "This will cover the costs, no?"

The thin man greedily snatched the coin out of the air, doing an especially poor job of hiding his excitement. "Yes, my lord. Of course, my lord."

"Good. Add the mother's body to the burn cart and then see to the boy. I want this dealt with before nightfall." The lord stopped at the threshold. "One more thing. The boy is now the property of the king. You know the punishment for stealing from the crown, correct?"

"Death, my lord," said the thin man. He began to lick at the back of his hands. Inexplicably, black hairs had started to sprout from his arms.

"I'm pleased we have an understanding," said the lord, not seeming to notice the thin man's transformation. He returned the bird mask to his face.

"*Squeak,*" said the thin man as he bowed to the departing lord. Demetry watched in bewilderment as the thin man's face slowly elongated into a snout. Whiskers sprung from his cheeks, and his two front teeth grew and grew until they dangled past his lower lip. He opened his mouth to speak but only a desperate pitiful squeak passed his lips.

"What witchcraft is this?" demanded Demetry in horror.

"*Squeak, squeak, squeak,*" replied the thin man, who now had the face of a rat. He lunged forward and bit Demetry on the nose.

Demetry returned to the waking world with a start. Sneak was standing on his face. Demetry sat bolt-upright in bed, his heart nearly leaping from his chest. Sneak gave a terrified squeak as she was sent catapulting through the air. She landed with a thump at the foot of his bed. This time, it was Demetry's turn to squeak in dismay.

"Sneak, what are you doing down here?" He kept his voice low to keep from waking Jeremiah. The rat scurried in hurried circles about Demetry's legs. He scooped her up in his hands. "What have you been up to?"

In truth, he knew the better part of that answer. Demetry hadn't seen the rat in over a year, but that didn't mean she wasn't often on the fringes of his mind. He would catch glimpses of her whereabouts when he slept — raiding the larder, exploring the other cell blocks, spying on Warden Cendrik and Chaplain Sighelm in their private chambers. It would seem Sneak had been very busy in the past year.

He stroked her black fur, finding that her little lungs were working especially hard. He intuitively understood why — Sneak had fled from someone down the stairwell.

"Jeremiah, wake up!" hissed Demetry, unable to hide the urgency in his voice. He quickly hid Sneak under his pillow.

Jeremiah was out of bed and on his feet in an instant. He snapped his fingers and the brazier flared to life, filling the chamber with light.

"There's someone coming," whispered Demetry. He could clearly hear footsteps now. *Clomp, tap, clomp.* That unsteady cadence belonged to only one man. The warden was coming to pay them a visit.

"Another letter?" wondered Demetry aloud. "But it's so soon."

Jeremiah looked equally perplexed.

Gong, gong, gong. Cendrik beat at the iron door with the head of his cane, causing the metal to ring so loudly it hurt Demetry's ears.

"Sir Jeremiah, we need to talk," called the warden. The friendly inflection that was normally present in his voice was missing.

Demetry and Jeremiah exchanged concerned looks.

"By all means," said Jeremiah, raising his voice to be heard through the closed door. "Why don't you step inside. We can have a conversation over breakfast."

Cendrik laughed, although it sounded forced and insincere. "Maybe another time. I think you would prefer to hear what I have to say in private." Cendrik reached through the narrow portal of the holding lock and dropped the gelding collar into the cell. "I'm sorry, but I'm not feeling especially trusting today. Jeremiah, if you would be so kind as to put on the collar."

Cendrik's face appeared on the far side of the holding lock, his lower lip glistening with drool. Jeremiah grunted discontentedly, but complied with the order. He locked the collar around his neck. Cendrik waited until he saw the Sundering Stone begin to glow before he withdrew from the portal. "And Demetry, please place your arm in the holding lock."

Jeremiah motioned for Demetry to do as he was

told. Demetry grumbled under his breath and grudgingly stuck his arm through the portal. His hand and wrist just barely reached the far side. Cendrik latched the iron cuff around Demetry's wrist, locking his arm fast. A wave of nausea rippled through Demetry's body as the Sundering Stone drank from his well of magic. He felt his knees buckle, and a sudden lightheadedness muddled his thoughts. It took all of his concentration to keep from vomiting.

The cell door unlocked and Jeremiah stepped outside. Demetry caught a brief glimpse of the two men standing alone in the dark corridor, then the door slammed shut sealing Demetry in his cell. Jeremiah and Cendrik walked off, leaving Demetry locked in place with his arm buried to the shoulder in the wall.

Demetry tried not to panic. This was the first time he had ever been alone in the cell. What if Jeremiah didn't return? What if they left him down here all alone for the rest of his life? What if? What if? What if? The thoughts entered his head, frantic and unwelcome. His heart began to gallop in his chest. He had to focus to slow down his breathing.

"*You're not alone. Not truly,*" reminded the voice in his head. Sneak clambered up Demetry's body and scurried down the length of his arm, joining

Jeremiah and Cendrik in the corridor.

Demetry closed his eyes, and suddenly he, too, was out in the corridor, hurrying along the ground on all fours. He kept to the shadows, his body pressed to the wall, his pupils dilated, looking for danger. The whiskers on his nose twitched as he sought out familiar scents. It didn't take long to find Jeremiah and Cendrik; they had only ascended to the first bend in the stairwell — just far enough that Demetry couldn't overhear their conversation.

The two men soared overhead like giants, their proportions distorted from Sneak's unnatural point of view. Demetry made his body — Sneak's body — motionless. The two men conversed quietly. Their words sounded foreign to Demetry's rat ears, yet somehow he comprehended everything that was said.

"It's time for you and I to be honest with one another," said Cendrik. He was leaning on his cane more than usual. His skin was pale, his face exhausted. "We're running out of time, Jeremiah. Our respective value to the king is wearing thin."

"How is the old fool doing?" asked Jeremiah. The Sundering Stone in Jeremiah's collar was glowing brightly, filling the stairwell with flickers of blue and green light.

"The king is growing old, growing impatient,

growing desperate. And as you and I both know, desperate men are prone to rash actions."

Jeremiah's eyes narrowed. "Don't make idle threats, Cendrik. If he lays a hand on her, I'll..."

"Do what? Go on a rampage? Burn Coljack to the ground? Set out on a vengeful vendetta to kill the king?" Cendrik shook his head. "Your threats are hollow, Jeremiah. The king's are not."

"I'll kill myself. Is that threat enough? I'll take the whereabouts of the Orb with me to the grave."

"There was a time when I would have taken that threat seriously. Not anymore. You've had years to swallow the bitter pill of death, yet you persist. Why? Because you are a survivor. Suicide is not in you. Besides, you wouldn't do anything that might put Princess Calycia's life in danger."

Demetry's little rat ears perked at the mention of the name. The Calycia sending Jeremiah letters was the princess? He suddenly had a hunch that the missing Orb wasn't the only reason Jeremiah was locked in prison. Romancing the heir's wife wasn't without consequences.

"You may be right," said Jeremiah. "You've known me longer than most. How many years has it been now?"

"It's been nearly fifteen years since I put a knife in your side," said Cendrik. "Does the wound still fester?"

Jeremiah shrugged off Cendrik's jab. "Fifteen years. That's a lifetime for some men. Tell me — in the intervening time, how many women have you loved, how many children have you reared? How often did you venture home to visit your family? Not once, right?" Jeremiah smiled like a wolf about to gorge on its prey. "You have paid a very high price for your loyalty to the throne."

If Jeremiah's mocking words were bothering him, Cendrik showed no sign. "I have paid a high price," he agreed. "But one day I will get my due reward."

"Ah, yes, after I let slip the location of the Orb." Jeremiah laughed. "A stubborn persistence — that is one thing you and I have in common. You still believe that the throne will reward you with a commission to the Academy Arcanum." Jeremiah shook his head. "The men you are counting on are snakes, more likely to kill you than give you a fair reward. But somewhere deep down, you must already know that, right?"

A corner of Cendrik's upper lip twitched, the only hint that Jeremiah's words had struck a nerve.

Jeremiah didn't let up. "You are as much a prisoner here as I am. And you know why? Dumb luck. You overheard a conversation not meant for your ears. You know that Princess Calycia does not love the prince. You know that she intended to run away from him on that fateful day in the woods. You know that she would sooner put a knife in his neck than live another day in his home. And how did Prince Rudlif cover his tracks? He whispered false praise in your ear, insisting that you alone had the ability to pierce my mind and discover the whereabouts of the Orb. But it was a lie. The truth is, you're not special, Cendrik. You're not Academy Arcanum material. You're not even a very good seer, to be honest. What you are, is a liability." He gave Cendrik's shoulder a sympathetic pat. "That's the problem with royals — they perceive all other lives as expendable. That's why I'm in prison. That's why you're in prison. And that's why neither of us are ever going to leave this place."

"You and I have one notable difference," said Cendrik, the hurt evident in his eyes.

"Oh, what's that?"

"The lie I tell myself still has a chance of coming true. Yours does not." His eyes narrowed. "That's why I came down here — I wanted you to hear the news from me. The princess will not be sending you any more letters."

The first flickers of fear began to show in Jeremiah's typically composed face. "What did he do to her?" Jeremiah hissed.

"Nothing," replied Cendrik. "But that didn't change her fate. This isn't a fairy tale, Jeremiah. None of us are immortal. Sometimes people die."

Jeremiah's brow furrowed. A dangerous glint entered his eyes. "You lie," he hissed after a lengthy moment of silence.

"Truly, I wish I did. I would like to think that your stubborn refusal to reveal the whereabouts of the Orb was for a worthwhile purpose, that you were engaged in some noble crusade to keep the woman you love alive. But here's the truth, your efforts at deception, your years of silent suffering, all were for nothing. Calycia is dead and there is nothing you could have done to prevent it."

This threw Jeremiah into a fit of rage. He lunged for Cendrik's neck, but the warden dodged aside, fast as a fish evading a predator. Jeremiah lunged again, but Cendrik, even with his disability, was able to dodge just out of reach.

"I may not be a very good seer, but I can still predict your every move," said Cendrik tapping at his own head. "You can reach left and I'll dodge right. We can play this game all day, but I'd rather not. I have never looked kindly on futility, and that is precisely the point you and I have reached in this journey. Calycia is gone — you can't protect her anymore."

"You lie," Jeremiah muttered again, but this time it was obvious he didn't mean the words. Although Jeremiah was trying to maintain his composure, Demetry could detect it cracking at the seams. His charcoal eyes, which were usually stoic, glinted with tears. His lips, usually drawn in a tight line, quivered with emotion.

Cendrik placed a hand on Jeremiah's shoulder, the gesture not unkind. "You've fought a good fight, but you've lost. Not to a spiteful old king or a crafty prison warden. You've lost to Fate. There is a plague sweeping the land. They are calling it the Breath of God. All who are afflicted die. If it's any consolation, Prince Rudlif is also amongst the dead."

Jeremiah's eyes showed no pleasure at the news. He stared at the floor, anguish eating at his heart.

"Jeremiah, I know this is painful, but I need you to keeping listening to me. The plague is just one of many ill tidings I bear. There are dragoons amassing north of the wall. War is coming. Capernicus is in danger. The Orb, Jeremiah, the king needs it."

Jeremiah swallowed the knot in his throat. "Who leads the dragoons?" he asked, his voice husky.

"No one knows for certain. Still, a man might

draw conclusions from the rumors — they say the leader is a creature of deep cunning and is worshiped by the other dragoons as a god."

"Tyronious." Jeremiah clutched at his chest.

"You know what must be done."

Jeremiah didn't answer. He suddenly appeared old and feeble. He grabbed the wall for support.

"I pray there is still a heart in there," said Cendrik, tapping on Jeremiah's chest. "Because only a heartless fool would ignore the perils that we face. The Orb is needed to protect the people, to protect your homeland from the reaching hand of our darkest foe. We need it."

Jeremiah shook his head. "No, the Orb was not meant for this purpose." A cold resolve entered his voice. "Calycia's life was your only bargaining chip. You have nothing. This conversation is through. Return me to my cell."

"There's a child, Jeremiah."

Jeremiah's eyes flared wide.

"I can speak nothing to the child's pedigree," continued Cendrik, "only that she is in her fourteenth year of life. How long have you been down here?" He sneered.

Jeremiah grabbed Cendrik by the neck. This time, the warden did nothing to dodge. Instead, he gave a low whistle and gestured downward with his eyes. He had a knife drawn to Jeremiah's midsection. "Make no mistake, there are still ways the king can hurt you. If you will not do your duty to the king, perhaps someone else will." He peered over Jeremiah's shoulder, down the passage toward the cell door. "What secrets have you told your young apprentice? What dark arts have you taught him? The king is always looking for skilled magics willing to serve."

Jeremiah released Cendrik's neck, a look of defeat in his eyes.

"Do you believe I put the boy in your cell on a whim?" asked Cendrik. "I've been looking for someone like Demetry since the day I arrived. Someone capable of the Old Magic. Someone who could break through your bristling coat of self-loathing. Someone you would be eager to foster and shape in your own image. Someone who could eventually rival you in their mastery of the dark arts." He gave Jeremiah a lopsided grin. "You may be interested to know that the boy has a vile history of self-preservation. If the king offered Demetry a hand, do you think he would refuse?"

Jeremiah did not answer, instead he stared at his feet and pawed at the gelding collar locked tight around his throat. "Get this damn thing off my neck and return me to my cell."

"Of course." Cendrik escorted Jeremiah back down the stairwell. "When I return tomorrow, you will tell me the whereabouts of the Orb. If you don't, I intend to take Demetry away from you. He is the king's property, after all." He removed the collar and shoved Jeremiah back into the cell.

Jeremiah kept his composure until the door slammed shut and the lock turned over. The telltale *step, clack, drag* of Cendrik's gait announced the warden's departure. As soon as Demetry and Jeremiah were alone, the elderly magic collapsed against the door gasping for breath.

"He lies. He lies," managed Jeremiah. His cheeks were tear-stained. Snot clumped in his beard. His chest heaved. Demetry had never seen Jeremiah look so frail, so defeated. "Calycia can't be dead. She can't be," Jeremiah kept repeating over and over again.

If there was one thing Demetry knew, it was that denial got men nowhere. He had gone that route with his mother and Joshua, and in each incident he had suffered the consequences. Right now, a hard decision had to be made and he needed Jeremiah thinking straight. They had precious little time before Cendrik returned.

Demetry took a knee beside his mentor, taking no pleasure in their reversal of roles. "I'm sorry,

Jeremiah, but Cendrik is likely telling the truth. Calycia forewarned of this possibility in her last letter, did she not?" He placed his arm around Jeremiah's heaving shoulders. "Plagues don't distinguish between rich or poor, highborn or low." The image of his mother's face blossomed in his mind, her eyes fixed, her pupils dilated, her skin blistered and pockmarked. Demetry shook his head — he had no time for self-pity right now.

Jeremiah didn't bother to ask how Demetry overheard the conversation. Perhaps he knew about the rat. Perhaps he didn't care. Demetry took Jeremiah's hand in his own, and for a long time they simply sat there in silence.

"Where did you hide the Orb?" asked Demetry, breaking the cardinal rule upon which their relationship was built. He expected Jeremiah to throw off his hold, to storm away in a fit of rage, to shout at Demetry for his insolence. Instead, Jeremiah simply sighed.

"Would you believe me if I told you I don't know where it's located?" said Jeremiah, his voice hardly a whisper. "I had to protect Calycia. Locked away in here I was helpless. Pretending to know the whereabouts of the Orb was the only ruse I had." He stared at the floor, his eyes brimming with fresh tears.

It took Demetry a moment to process the information. "If you don't know the Orb's location, you have lost all of your bargaining power." He gasped. "What about Calycia's daughter? Do you think the king will hurt her?"

"If what Cendrik said is true, the child is the king's only heir. He won't touch her. He can't, not without the risk of ruining his own legacy. If the king plans to use someone against me, it is most likely going to be you, Demetry. He will make you an offer that will be difficult to refuse — a pardon in exchange for an oath of fealty. He will need a warrior with your unique abilities if he is to have any hope of defeating the dragoons in the coming war."

Demetry had never considered that before. His skills might buy him his freedom, but it would come at a dire cost — he would have to betray Jeremiah to a life of solitude in the depths of Coljack.

"I thought I could protect Calycia with a lie, but I failed," said Jeremiah, with a sad shake of his head. "Perhaps I can do better with you."

"What do you mean?"

"When Cendrik returns I want you to tell him that you are ready to talk. When in private, inform him that you know where the Orb is located."

Demetry raised his eyebrow circumspectly. "And where would this Orb be hidden?"

"In Luthuania. Tell him the elves have it."

Demetry nodded his head, understanding the play at hand. "The best lies are the ones that can not be proven wrong."

"Indeed. This little fib might be enough to buy you your freedom."

Demetry looked to Jeremiah, sensing the sincerity in the man's face. Jeremiah was willing to sacrifice himself so that Demetry could be free. But right now, Jeremiah was hurt, and he was making a grave choice while still reeling from the news of his loved one's death. Demetry could never accept an offer made under such conditions, could he?

A cold laughter filled his head. *"You promised you would not falter or flinch if the opportunity to escape arose."* Joshua's voice was bitter and mocking. *"You're not turning craven, are you?"*

That was before I had someone other than myself to care about, thought Demetry in reply. *That was before someone gave a damn about me. I can't turn my back on Jeremiah. Family members protect each other.*

"You believe you can escape your sins, Demetry, but you're wrong. What you did to Shep and me in the woods wasn't an anomaly. It's who you are."

You were a mistake, thought Demetry. *A rash*

decision made by a rash child, who didn't comprehend the consequences of his actions. I will not repeat my error.

Joshua squealed in protest.

Demetry shook his head, silencing the objecting voice in his head. He rose to his feet, steadfast with resolve. "I will not sacrifice you for my own freedom," declared Demetry, rejecting Jeremiah's plan outright. He grabbed Jeremiah by the crook of his arm and helped him to his feet. "If I'm getting out of here, I'm not going alone. Both of us go, or both of us stay."

Jeremiah ran his hands along the stone buttresses flanking the door. "I've lived in this room for over a decade. Don't you think I've thought this through? It's not possible."

"That might have been true when you were locked in here by yourself. But now there are two of us." *Or three, or four, depending on how you count.* Demetry knocked on the iron door. "What if I can get them to open the door for us?"

"Say you could. We would still have the battering ram and the flood water to contest with."

Demetry smirked devilishly. "I already have the battering ram covered." Sneak scurried across the floor and clambered up Demetry's back. She squatted obediently on his shoulder. He rewarded her with a scratch behind the ears. "Here's a interesting tidbit Chaplain Sighelm once told me — did you know a man can lose a quarter of his blood before succumbing to his wounds?" Demetry collected an empty waste pail from the corner of the room. "Tonight, you and I are going to test that theory."

CHAPTER
X

FIGHT AND FLIGHT

The boy is dead! Take him away!" Jeremiah's voice rumbled from the depths of the earth, reverberating through the halls of Coljack and stirring the guards from their sleep.

Sneak wrinkled her nose as she watched them come, a dozen men all wearing the yellow robes of the Yanish Brotherhood. They came snaking down the stairwell in a silent column, their faces illuminated by orange torchlight. No one appeared eager to respond to Jeremiah's call. By the time they reached the bottom of the stairwell their brows were slick with sweat and their shirts soaked through.

The first brother to reach the cell door wiped the sweat out of his eyes as he hunched over to peer through the portal. "The gods help me," sputtered the man, as he recoiled in horror from what he saw.

"What is it?" The next man stomached the sight little better. He doubled over and began to hyperventilate, his skin turning pale.

Demetry's body lay butchered in the center of the prison cell. His blood painted the walls and floor, staining the whole interior red.

Jeremiah's maddened voice rang clearly in the corridor. "Bring me another, Cendrik. Are you out there? Can you hear me? Bring me another and we'll try again. Isn't that what you want?"

A curse sounded from the rear of the column of Yanish Brothers. Chaplain Sighelm emerged, shouldering his way to the front of the pack. Cupping his hands about his face, he peered through the portal. Jeremiah was standing in the middle of the chamber. His hair was in disarray. The right sleeve of his robe was ripped at the shoulder. Jeremiah's desk was toppled over and his papers, which he typically kept so fastidiously organized, were thrown about the room. Burn marks blackened the walls, and Demetry's mattress was scorched and pockmarked with holes. Sighelm traced the mayhem with his eyes.

"What happened, Jeremiah?" pressed Sighelm, his voice purposefully tempered and cool.

Jeremiah jutted his chin toward Demetry's body,

his lips twitching with rage. "Tell Cendrik his little ruse didn't work. I'm no fool. The boy was a spy. He confessed to everything before I was done with him." He had his arms crossed behind his back, purposefully keeping his hands hidden from view.

"Let me see your hands, Jeremiah."

"Curse you, Sighelm. Send for the warden."

"The warden is sleeping. You have to deal with me instead."

"Asleep, or is Cendrik too much of a coward to face me?"

Sighelm didn't bother to answer. "Show me your hands."

Jeremiah lifted his hands above his head. They were stained red to the wrists. A piece of sharpened stone was clutched in his fist.

Sighelm frowned. "Put the weapon down and place your arm in the holding lock."

"Why don't you come in here and make me?" The cell darkened, the torches in the corridor guttered and threatened to extinguish. The men looked about themselves in terror. Only Sighelm seemed unfazed.

"He's gone mad," whispered one of the brothers, crossing himself.

Sighelm shook his head. "No. Cendrik fucked up. We had a good thing going. I told him not to push the matter, to be patient, but he wouldn't wait."

"The Proconsul is going to be pissed," muttered one of the men.

"No shit," said Sighelm. He spit on the ground and turned his attention back to the interior of the cell.

Jeremiah was pacing back and forth, like a bear trapped in a cage.

"I'll give you two options. Drop the weapon and place your hand in the holding lock..."

"Or?"

"Or I'll leave Demetry's body in there until graveworms are crawling from his eyes and his body splits open with rot. Have you ever smelled a decomposing body?"

"More than I could count." Jeremiah sneered like a madman. He momentarily slipped from view, only to reappear with his face flush against the portal. "I curse you for forcing my hand. The boy didn't deserve this. You used my compassion against me." He pointed toward Demetry, his finger quivering. "Take him away. A corpse shares no secrets with the living."

Jeremiah shoved his arm through the holding lock and waved his hand about until Sighelm locked the iron fetter around his wrist. Sighelm waited until the Sundering Stone set in the fetter was glowing brightly before turning his attention back to his men.

"Swiftfeld and Wulgan, you're coming with me to fetch the body. Hother and Ethel, put a blade to Jeremiah's neck. If he gives you reason to strike, don't hesitate. The rest of you stay in the corridor. If things go bad, sound the alarm."

"But they'll flood the corridor," said a big man from the rear of the group. He had a ram's horn slung over his shoulder.

"Better that than have Sir Jeremiah on the loose, I promise you," said Sighelm.

The big man chuckled. "Jeremiah's arm is secure in the holding lock. The Sundering Stone has him gelded. He's not going anywhere."

"Myer, I know you are accustomed to dealing with prisoners who are as dumb as you are, so let me make this very clear. Sir Jeremiah is smarter than you, he's deadlier than you, and he's pissed off. Give him an inch and you'll be picking your teeth out of the back of your skull. So if I say sound the alarm, place your lips to the end of that horn and blow until you're blue in the face. Got it?"

Myer nodded dumbly and held his horn up and at the ready.

Sighelm thrust his thumb toward the door. "Let's go." He unlocked the cell door and the men rushed inside. The difference in temperature between the corridor and the cell was impossible to ignore. The men immediately began to shiver.

"The gods help me, it's freezing in here," murmured one of the brothers, his breath blossoming in a cloud of white vapor.

"Shut up and get into position," ordered Sighelm. He led two men to collect Demetry's blood-drenched body, while the other two men tended to Jeremiah. The elderly magic was stuck in the holding lock, his entire left arm buried in the wall. He posed a threat to no one. Still, the guards weren't taking any chances. Hother, the younger of the Yanish Brothers, placed a dagger to Jeremiah's throat.

"The gods favor those who respect their elders," said Jeremiah, moving his lower jaw as little as possible to keep the dagger from digging into his flesh. "The things I know could make a man quite rich. Why don't you step outside and uncuff me. I will not forget your kindness."

"Don't hesitate to kill him if he gives you cause," reiterated Sighelm, as he wove his way through the gore strewn cell. The floor was sticky with coagulated blood — there was no way to avoid it.

"Get his legs," instructed Sighelm. He grabbed Demetry's wrists and lifted.

Demetry waited until he felt his body leave the ground. Waited until he heard the men grunting from exertion. Waited until they got him close to the door. His heart raced. Just a few more steps and they would be out in the corridor, then Demetry would give them a show they would never forget.

"He can't have been dead for long," said one of the brothers carrying Demetry's leg. "His body's still warm."

Demetry cursed in his head. *Keep walking. Keep walking.*

"What's a rat doing way down here?" called one of the brothers standing at the cell door.

There was a high pitched squeak, followed by a sickening crunch and the sound of a boot heel digging into the ground.

"A rat?" wondered Sighelm aloud. Demetry felt Sighelm's hand readjust, his fingers sliding toward the middle of Demetry's wrist. Sighelm pressed down hard on the artery, searching for a pulse.

A quiet gasp passed Sighelm's lips.

Demetry couldn't wait any longer. He thrust open his eyelids, locking eyes with Sighelm. "I've been waiting for you," Demetry hissed.

Sighelm recoiled in shock and released Demetry's wrists. Demetry swung earthward like a dropped pendulum. His head cracked hard against the floor. The two Yanish Brothers holding Demetry's legs were slower to react. They both stared at Demetry with dumbfounded expressions, their mouths hanging wide open. Demetry didn't give them time to figure out what was happening. He channeled the Sundered Soul and created a void in the air behind either man, and just like that, the Old Magic took hold of their bodies, sending the two men careening in opposite directions through the chamber.

Sighelm stabbed down with the butt end of his club, intending to crack Demetry's skull wide open. Demetry rolled aside. The steel shaft slammed against the floor, sending chips of stone flying. Sighelm swung again. With no time to dodge, Demetry used his forearm as a shield. At the last second he envisioned the bones in his arm taking on the strength of iron. The club struck. The flesh in Demetry's forearm split open from the force of the blow, but the bones withstood the impact.

"The Old Magic is yours to command," whispered Joshua, cheering him on. *"Kill them all!"*

Demetry lunged forward and seized Sighelm's

ankle.

"Shut the door!" yelled Sighelm. He pummeled Demetry's back with his club, but it had no effect — Demetry's grip was as strong as an iron vice.

"Do you want the blade or the fire?" asked Demetry, remembering the time Sighelm gave him the same choice. He didn't wait for a reply. Flames leapt up Sighelm's leg, boiling over his clothes and licking at his exposed skin. He shrieked in terror. Demetry released Sighelm from his grasp and turned his attention to the two Yanish Brothers holding blades to Jeremiah's neck.

The men in the corridor were waving their arms, urging their comrades to flee. One brother abandoned his post and sprinted for the door. The other seemed conflicted, his attention divided between Jeremiah, Demetry, and the human torch that was rolling around on the floor.

"You should have let me loose when you had the chance," said Jeremiah to the Yanish Brother. "A pity."

The man opened his mouth, perhaps to say a word, but only a scream came out. He went shooting across the room, dragged forward by the midsection as if someone had lassoed a rope around his waist. His arm passed through the threshold just as the men in the hallway were pulling the cell door shut. There was a sickening crack as the iron door slammed on the man's wrist. Demetry had intended to block the passage with the man's body, but an arm served just as well. The door swung back open with a reverberating twang. The men in the hall kept trying to close the door, slamming it over and over again on the poor man's arm. Their panic-stricken minds were oblivious to what was keeping the door ajar.

Sighelm crawled toward the door, the lower half of his body in flames. Black smoke pooled on the ceiling, filling the room with the stench of charred flesh. "Sound the alarm, open the floodgate!" he croaked. His last words. He curled fetal and didn't move again. The nobility of Sighelm's final act wasn't lost on Demetry.

"A worthwhile foe."

Demetry nodded his head in agreement.

The men in the corridor gave up trying to shut the door and ran. The Yanish Brother with the broken arm wallowed in the threshold, grabbing his shattered wrist. Myer, the man tasked with sounding the alarm, seemed incapable of moving. His eyes were as wide as saucers as he slowly lifted the ram's horn to his lips and blew. A shrill blast echoed up the spiral stairwell, sounding his own doom. That seemed to break the spell that kept him frozen in place. He fled up the stairwell, bowling over anyone who got in his way. The other men followed, a frantic stampede to reach the landing before the battering ram fell and the water came rushing down.

Unhurried, Demetry stepped out into the corridor. He felt especially pleased with how events had unfolded. Jeremiah and Demetry had spent the previous day taking turns bleeding into the bucket. By the time they were finished painting the walls and floors red, they were both lightheaded from blood loss. It was Jeremiah's idea to blast the room with incendiary spells — it made the story Jeremiah told the guards all the more believable.

He found Sneak's body in the corridor. She crawled toward Demetry, her back legs dragging uselessly in her wake. "Farewell, my friend," said Demetry, giving Sneak's ears one final scratch. "It's time for you to return to your eternal slumber." He released Sneak's body from his spell, and she immediately went limp. She was an unfortunate casualty, but the rat had been expendable from the start. He would not shed tears over a creature that had died long ago. Even so, he felt a lump rise in his throat.

Feeling somewhat embarrassed, he quickly unlocked the iron fetter from around Jeremiah's wrist, being especially careful not to touch the Sundering Stone, and then hurried back into the cell. He found Jeremiah leaning wearily against the wall.

"I never get used to it," said Jeremiah, rubbing at his wrist. There were burn marks where the Sundering Stone had made contact with his bare flesh. "I've been able to channel the Sundered Soul for as long as I can remember. When that power is stripped away, it's like I'm missing a part of myself."

Demetry knew the feeling all too well. He wrapped his arm around Jeremiah's back and guided him toward the cell door. "We need to keep moving," said Demetry. "It will only be a matter of time until Cendrik learns of our escape." He collected a discarded torch and held it aloft to illuminate the path.

Jeremiah climbed the stairs in silence, his face curled in contemplation. Demetry could scarcely imagine the thoughts going through the old man's head. After well over a decade in captivity, freedom was just beyond the bend. Of course, they weren't free, not yet. Demetry half-expected a flood of water to come pouring down the stairwell at any moment. They needed to hurry — the guards wouldn't delay forever.

Up, up, up they went, past collapsed mine shafts and dark tunnels that led nowhere. The stairwell seemed to go on forever. The ascent was taking far longer than planned. A cold sweat embraced Demetry's body. He never realized how deep in the earth they actually were. He may have miscalculated.

"*Have faith in the plan*," chided Joshua.

"Damn this place," said Demetry, trying to distract himself from his fraying nerves. He began to list off every person who had ever done him wrong, finding determination in his hatred. "Damn Cendrik. Damn the king. Damn Shep, and Hanberg, and Headmaster Rioley. Damn the school elders, and the magistrate who sent me to Taper in the first place."

"Don't forget to damn yourself," said Jeremiah, breathing hard. "It was your own failings that got you imprisoned here. Don't ever forget that."

"I won't," said Demetry.

"*We won't,*" said the voice in his head.

The truth was, Demetry was terrified. He was terrified of what might await them at the top of the stairwell, or outside the prison fortress, or beyond in the world at large. Powerful forces had conspired to put him in prison. Even if he escaped, he would spend the rest of his life as a hunted man. His only advantage would be his magic.

"Yes, but will it be enough?"

Demetry wasn't certain. Jeremiah had taught him more in the past year than he would have learned in a lifetime of study at Taper. But such knowledge didn't make him invincible. A trained battlemage from the Academy Arcanum would likely be more than Demetry could handle. Even a bowman with a lucky shot could end his life. Still, Jeremiah had given him a fighting chance and Demetry couldn't be more grateful.

"Jeremiah, what you've done — taking me under your wing and all. Well, I..." His voice cracked and he found himself blinking back tears. Demetry had never been very good at putting his feelings into words, and now was no different. How could Demetry explain to Jeremiah that he was more than a mentor or a friend? Jeremiah had become the closest thing to a father Demetry had ever known. "I'm grateful for everything."

"Hold you sniffling for now," said Jeremiah, his voice having regained its typical authoritative tone. "Your trial is not yet through."

There was a commotion around the next bend. Demetry silently thanked the gods. They arrived to the landing. But now came his true test. The guards had ample time to prepare. Demetry envisioned fire in his mind's eye and leapt onto the landing expecting a fight.

Instead of being confronted by a host of armed guards, they were greeted by a pair of terrified Yanish Brothers. The two men were frantically trying to dislodge the lynch pin that held the battering ram in place. They yelped in terror when Demetry and Jeremiah emerged from around the corner and abandoned their post. Demetry motioned to stop them, but Jeremiah held him back.

"Let them go."

Demetry grunted with frustration, but followed his elder's command. He walked over to the battering ram's lynch pin, eager to examine Sneak's handiwork.

The lynch pin and the two eyelets through which it passed were corroded together, forming a single ugly hunk of rusted iron. Clyde's antics with the door hinge had given Demetry the idea. Sneak had done the deed. The rat had been paying the battering ram a daily visit for nearly a year. Rat piss could do wonders when it came to corroding iron. Demetry couldn't have been more pleased with the result.

He cupped his hands around the lynch pin and channeled the Sundered Soul. The metal instantaneously turned white hot as he excited the individual particles within the beam. It turned to fluid in his hands, spilling between his fingers in glowing tendrils. There was a twang, and the heavy chain holding the battering ram in place broke free. The iron-tipped ram, which had hung motionless for over a decade, finally fulfilled its purpose. It slammed into the far wall with a deafening boom. Black cracks cobwebbed across the surface. Jets of water sprayed from the fissures, growing larger with every passing moment. Demetry and Jeremiah stepped aside, and the wall came tumbling down. Water rushed through the gap, a boiling tempest. Down, down, down it went, galloping along the steps in a frothing current no man could contest. If anyone remained below, they were doomed.

"Why did you do that?" asked Jeremiah, watching the water rush by. He leaned against the wall, exhausted from the ascent, pale from blood loss, and weak from the Sundering Stone.

"I'm not going back into the cell, not ever," said Demetry, spitting into the current. "If Cendrik captures me, he's going to have to kill me."

Coljack was a maze, but after more than a year of witnessing the world through Sneak's eyes, Demetry knew the passages by heart. He quickly guided them toward the front gate, walking through ominously empty halls. Every guard post they passed was abandoned. The barracks they walked through were empty. Every bed was in disarray. Prisoners banged on their cell doors as Demetry and Jeremiah entered the final corridor, yelling praises and condemnations, encouragement and curses.

"We should free these men from their cells," said Demetry, envisioning the chaos that would ensue.

Jeremiah shook his head. "Most of these men deserve to be here."

"Did I? Did you?"

Jeremiah didn't respond, he didn't need to. Demetry already knew the answer. *Yes.*

They stepped outside.

The walls of Coljack were black shadows against the backdrop of the night sky. The courtyard was barren. The battlements and surrounding towers were not. Every guard in the Coljack garrison was present, men with drawn bows, pointed spears, and terrified faces. More guards were gathered atop the east and west towers. Only one figure seemed calm amongst the rest. Warden Cendrik strode to the front of the battlement, leaning wearily upon his cane. His lips curled in that half-smirk expression he so often wore.

"Impressive, gentlemen," said Cendrik. He gave them a mocking clap. "You thwarted all of my fail-safes. But now you face the true test." He pointed his cane toward Jeremiah. "It would seem the master is at a disadvantage. The Sundering Stone drank all of his strength."

Jeremiah didn't refute the claim, and even if he did, everyone would have seen it was a lie. Jeremiah's eyes were sagging and bloodshot, his breathing labored. He had to lean against Demetry for support. Demetry cursed under his breath. This was one part of the plan Demetry hadn't thought through. They should have lingered awhile longer in Coljack — that would have granted Jeremiah more time to recover.

Cendrik nodded toward Demetry. "That leaves the young apprentice to pick up the slack. Are you up to the task, Demetry? I once saw Jeremiah deflect the shots of a dozen bowmen with his powers. Let's see how you compare."

He tapped the tip of his cane into the ground. That was the signal the archers were waiting for. They let loose all at once. In the blink of an eye, there were more projectiles in the air than Demetry could count, let alone manipulate with his magic. Demetry's first impulse was to duck, but knew such cowardly instincts would only get him killed. Magic was their only hope.

Demetry turned his focus to the cloudless night sky. A downdraft of air came collapsing out of the heavens, striking the arrows mid-flight. The sudden gust redirected most of the shafts into the ground, but a few managed to stay on mark. They slammed into the wall, missing Jeremiah and Demetry by only inches.

"Again!" ordered Cendrik, his lips still upturned in a grin.

Demetry was more prepared for the second attack. This time a crosswind sent every arrow sailing wide of its mark. He didn't let the archers fire a third time.

Demetry turned his attention to the wooden gate that barred their path. In his mind's eye, he envisioned the millions of water particles that resided within the planks of wood. Individually, each particle was minuscule and irrelevant. Collectively, they were packed with potential energy. He clapped his hands, turning the water particles to ice. He clapped again, and the ice turned to gas. The resulting blast was catastrophic. Instead of just destroying the wooden gate, the entire gatehouse was torn apart, sending rocks and mortar flying through the air.

Half the men atop the battlements were

knocked off their feet. More still were dazed by the concussion of the blast. No one was more surprised than Demetry. This time it was Jeremiah who sprung into action first.

"Keep your head low!" ordered Jeremiah, as he pulled Demetry along by the collar. They ducked and ran as bricks tumbled from the sky. The gatehouse had been reduced to a pile of debris no taller than a man in height. They clambered over the ruins. The guards atop the battlements were just starting to regain their composure when Demetry and Jeremiah reached the far side of the debris field. More arrows flew, but this time their aim was haphazard, parting shots fired by men who knew they were bested. Demetry glanced over his shoulder one last time in hopes of spotting Warden Cendrik. The warden was nowhere to be seen.

"Hopefully the bastard took a brick to the face," whispered Joshua.

Demetry smiled at the thought.

They sprinted into the farmland that lay beyond the walls of the fortress prison. Ripe crops were arranged in neat rows — golden brown grains, grapes swollen on the vine. The scents of summer were heavy on the air. Crickets chirped, night birds and bats whirled overhead hunting for insects. Demetry couldn't imagine a more perfect scene to welcome him back into the world. He had never known such joy. He leapt from furrow to furrow, hollering triumphantly at the night sky. Jeremiah trailed behind him, no more hurried than ever. The torchlights atop the battlements grew further and further away, eventually becoming faint specks on the horizon.

"Can you believe what I did back there?" Demetry wasn't being boastful. He was genuinely shocked by his own power. Out of necessity, his full strength had always been held back within the confines of the prison cell. Now that he had seen the magnitude of his true power he was flabbergasted.

"We can stop now, Demetry," called Jeremiah. He was slowly making his way over the final hump of farmland. "They won't be coming after us anytime soon. Look."

In the distance, Coljack burned. The amber glow of fire perfectly outlined the jagged teeth of the battlements. The wind carried with it the faint ring of alarm bells and the frantic cries of men.

Fate works in mysterious ways, thought Demetry.

Perhaps a lantern had been knocked over in the confusion, or maybe a torch had been flung from the battlements and into a pile of hay. Or perhaps Cendrik had started the blaze to hide the folly of his own error. Either way, the fortress prison was burning. Demetry could only take so much delight from the sight — most of the structure was mortar and stone, and everything else could be rebuilt. He thought of the men trapped inside only as an afterthought.

"I... I need to rest," said Jeremiah. He was struggling to catch his breath. "I'm too old to be running aimlessly in the night." Jeremiah's face was oddly sedate for someone who had just escaped prison. He ran his hand slowly over the stalks of grain, letting them tickle the tips of his fingers. He smiled faintly, then stumbled to his knees as his legs gave out beneath him.

Demetry gasped and ran to his mentor's side, arriving just in time to catch his fall. Demetry's hand struck something jagged and damp as he secured Jeremiah's frame in his arms. His stomach knotted. He gingerly ran his fingers over the finely sharpened metallic head and the wooden shaft. His blood ran cold. An arrow protruded from Jeremiah's back through his right shoulder.

"You've been struck," managed Demetry. He nearly choked on the words. "My magic should have protected you."

"Yet it did not," said Jeremiah. He smiled foolishly. "You've done well, Demetry. I can ask nothing more."

Demetry cradled Jeremiah's frail body while he searched for a healing spell that might suffice. He came up with nothing. He would have to use the Old Magic. He ripped open Jeremiah's shirt and examined the wound. Based on the point of entry the arrow had pierced Jeremiah's right lung. Demetry tried to envision the organs in his mind. Spongy and fibrous. Replete with arteries. Rich with blood.

Jeremiah steadied Demetry's trembling hand. "Wait a moment and look at the stars with me," said Jeremiah. He was struggling to keep his voice calm.

"There's no time," said Demetry, feeling panic take hold. Healers practiced for years, honing their skills on animals, studying the anatomy of cadavers, learning the functions of the organs and the layout of bones and muscles. Demetry would have to rely on instinct alone.

"There's always time for a moment," said Jeremiah, coughing between words. Flecks of blood landed in his beard. His breath turned into a pitiful wheeze. Jeremiah was dying before Demetry's eyes and there was nothing he could do.

"See how they shine," said Jeremiah, his voice now a whisper. He turned Demetry's chin, forcing him to stare skyward. "Isn't it outstanding?"

It truly was. The stars were brighter than Demetry ever remembered. Every constellation was on proud display. The evening star glittered in the west, while the great serpent streaked from horizon to horizon. The beauty caused Demetry's breath to catch in his throat. "You're right, it truly is outstanding."

There was no response.

Demetry remained at Jeremiah's side, his heart broken with grief. The pain was paralyzing, and for a long time he could do nothing, save stare into the face of the man he had loved like a father. Jeremiah's flesh gradually became pale, and then cold. Eventually, all semblance of life slipped away.

"You betrayed me." Demetry sniffed and wiped away the onset of a tear. "You're selfish. You know that, right? The whole world is out to get me and you've left me alone. I can't do this by myself."

As he talked, the field was embraced by a wicked chill. His anger got the better of him, and he subconsciously summoned the Sundered Soul. Demetry didn't care, he let his rage take his mind were it would. The waving stalks of grain that surrounded him began to freeze solid and snap in half like icicles. His breath issued from his mouth in clouds of vapor. The earth became rock hard.

His clothing became stiff and shrouded with frost. Demetry would have been satisfied to sit there until he froze to death, but the voices in his head were not so eager to surrender.

"*They're coming*," hissed Joshua.

Dogs barked in the distance. The flames in Coljack were extinguished. Shadowy figures gathered before the battlement walls, while to the east the sun peeked over the lip of the world. He didn't have much time.

Demetry leaned over and kissed Jeremiah's brow. "I'm not abandoning you, but I have to go." he whispered into his mentor's ear. "I'm sorry."

With eyes shrouded in tears, Demetry turned his back on his old life, and went racing from the field. He was now sadly certain his sins would haunt him to the grave.

CHAPTER
XI

HEROES AND VILLAINS

Demetry scrambled up the hill, his feet slipping in the mud. The hounds barked and howled in the valley below as they galloped in pursuit. A horn blared to the south. A replying cry sounded to the north. They would be on him soon. Demetry almost didn't care. He hadn't slept in days. His muscles ached, and his arms and legs were covered in scrapes and bruises from falling. Even his bones seemed to hurt. He couldn't keep at this pace much longer. A fight today would at least put an end to all this running. It was almost a comforting thought.

Demetry set out from Coljack with a single destination in mind — the elven border. His failure to flee to Luthuania after Joshua's death had cost him almost two years of his life. He wasn't about to make the same mistake twice.

Demetry had entered the mountainous territory that lay between Luthuania and Capernicus two days prior. It was disputed land, and only the most foolhardy entered the territory. Demetry assumed his pursuers would turn back once he entered the foothills of the Eng Mountains. He had no such luck.

As Demetry made his ascent, Cendrik's hunting party pressed on right behind him. Each night, Demetry spotted the campfires of his pursuers and marked their progress. They were a day behind him. Then a few miles. Then so close he could count the men as they milled about in their camp.

Cendrik's hunting party had turned into a small army over the course of the journey. Each day they drew closer, and each day more men joined the pack. Men on horseback hemmed Demetry in. Men with hounds haunted his every step. But the foes Demetry truly feared were the last two men to join Cendrik's host. They came richly attired, dressed in bright silks and wearying gaudy gemstones around their necks. These were the trappings of a Academy Arcanum graduate. The men were battlemages, Demetry imagined, sent by the king to finish the job.

Jeremiah had made Demetry powerful, capable of using a form of magic few could scarcely comprehend. But these men were trained killers. In a few years Demetry might be able to contest a battlemage spell for spell, but right now he was outmatched and outnumbered.

"If I reach the far side of the range they'll have to turn back," muttered Demetry to himself, as he forged a path through a silent forest of evergreens and dead pine needles. The summit loomed close, mockingly so, a bare slap of weathered granite, naked save for the few patches of snow that still clung to its southern face. One more day and he would surmount the summit. Of course, that depended on his strength not giving out first.

This was likely all part of Cendrik's plan. The warden was toying with Demetry, letting him wear himself ragged. Demetry had the sick impression the seer could predict his every move. It was like playing a game of bones with an opponent who already knew the final tally — there was no contest, just a slow and steady slog toward an unavoidable conclusion.

Hand over hand, step after step, Demetry climbed higher. His pursuers were so close he could hear their muffled voices as they called to one another coordinating movements. The main hunting party was right behind him, smaller groups were creeping up his flanks. Demetry shook his head. He was tired of running, tired of being outplayed. He found a flat rock near a stream and sat down. This seemed as good a place as any to make his stand. It seemed as good a place as any to die.

The sun slowly shifted across the sky. They would be upon him soon.

"Are you really going to sit here and wait for them to come and kill you?" Joshua's voice sounded especially shrill in his head.

"Why should I keep running?" said Demetry. "There's no grand prize at the end of this path. Everything I have ever cared about is behind me. My mother. My home. Jeremiah."

"Don't fool yourself, Demetry. You never had anyone to begin with. Your existence has been lonely and bitter from the start. That is, until you found me."

"You misjudge me."

"Do I? I'm a part of you now. I can see your deepest thoughts, I know your darkest sins."

Demetry snorted. "You are my darkest sin. I should have never raised you from the dead. You haunt me like a vengeful specter, whispering lies and vile advice in my ear."

A shrill laughter filled his head. *"Haunt you? I empower you. I tell you the things you need to hear. I make sure you're not controlled by cowardice. Think of all we have done together. We have learned to Channel the Sundered Soul. We have mastered the dark art of the Old Magic. We have escaped the inescapable confines of Coljack and left a path of ruin in our wake. We have become akin to gods."*

Demetry beat at his head with his fists, trying to quiet the nagging voice. "I'm sorry I brought you on this journey. What's dead is dead. I should have let you rest in peace."

Joshua didn't respond.

Footsteps sounded in the surrounding woods, the familiar *clomp, tap, clomp* Demetry had grown to loathe.

"Who are you talking to, Demetry?"

Warden Cendrik was standing near the stream leaning upon his cane for support. His men were silently fanning out, fencing Demetry in with a wall of leveled blades and drawn bows.

"Why won't you let me escape?" asked Demetry. The tone of his voice bordered on pleading. "How many men must I kill before you will leave me alone? How many lives am I worth?"

"To me, very few," admitted Cendrik. "But to the king you have grown quite valuable. A man capable of controlling the Old Magic is rare indeed. The throne has been looking for someone with your talents for decades."

Demetry spit. "The king couldn't control

Jeremiah, why does he think he can control me?"

"He doesn't," said Cendrik, pawing aside the drool that was pooling at the corner of his lips. "But he believes you can be bargained with. Jeremiah was old and set in his ways, his heart filled with vengeance and self-vindication. He was as unyielding as the ancient oak in a storm — he would break before he bent. But you are the willow, Demetry. The wind blows and you bend to accommodate. That shows a sensibility. Your young mind understands how the world really works. Give and take, my friend, that is the cornerstone of any healthy relationship."

Demetry's eyes narrowed with suspicion. Kind words spoken by a snake were no less dangerous than a threat. Still, Demetry couldn't help but feel intrigued. "What is the king willing to give and what is he eager to take?"

"How would you like a new life?" asked Cendrik, shuffling closer. "Free of prison. Free of being hunted. Perhaps even an appointment to the Academy Arcanum. You are eager to finish honing your skills, are you not? You could become the king's greatest champion, defender of the realm, court magic, even. These are no small titles, especially for a lad born into poverty."

Demetry sneered. "I'm a killer. I'm a

necromancer."

Cendrik waved off Demetry's claims. "Your past crimes are nothing to the king. Your powers are all he cares about. Bow in fealty before the Throne of Caper, swear your allegiance to the king and you will be reborn!"

Demetry envisioned the future that might be. No more fear. No more want. A clean slate upon which he could build his life. Graduates of the Academy Arcanum were held in the highest esteem. They became the advisers of lords, the commanders of armies, and in some cases the rulers of their own fiefdoms. It was a life Demetry had never dreamed possible, not since that unfortunate day when Joshua died and Demetry's world was turned upside down.

"But full repentance comes at a cost," said Cendrik stepping closer. "What did your mentor do with the Orb?"

For once Demetry saw no reason to lie. "Jeremiah never actually knew the whereabouts of the Orb. It was all a ploy to protect the woman he loved."

Cendrik lifted his brow incredulously. "Then the old man lied to you." He tapped at his head. "I'm a seer, remember. I can see into a man's soul. Jeremiah went to great lengths to protect his secrets. His mind was like a black well. Even I had a hard time piercing his veil of shadow and guile, but in moments of weakness a glimmer showed through. I have seen him holding the Orb with my mind's eye. I know he was there the day it was stolen from the king. Search your memory, Demetry. There has to be something he let slip."

Demetry racked his brain, trying to think of everything Jeremiah had shared about his past life. Where he had lived, what he had done, who he had served, and betrayed, and loved. He came up empty-handed. Jeremiah had instructed Demetry to tell Cendrik the Orb was hidden in Luthuania, but that lie seemed wholly insufficient given the current circumstances — Cendrik's intuition would see he wasn't telling the truth. "I can't think of anything," Demetry finally admitted.

Cendrik's eyes narrowed. "You lie as well as the old man, but your mind betrays you. There's something you're hiding from me." He edged closer, his hand reaching toward Demetry's face.

Demetry's head began to throb. His thoughts became confused, irrational.

"The Orb..."

"Tell me..."

"Where...."

Cendrik was using his powers to invade

Demetry's mind and search for the truth. Demetry backed away and swatted at the air, as if that might dislodge Cendrik's mental grasp.

"Pay the final price for your repentance, Demetry." Cendrik pressed forward, his eyes pinched shut, his lopsided face twitching with concentration. "A new life awaits you. All you have to do is tell me where the Orb is hidden."

"All you have to do is let me in."

The pressure in Demetry's skull intensified. His thoughts became muddled, confused. Demetry tried to think of a way to contest Cendrik's probing powers, but the Old Magic was elemental in nature. Demetry could manipulate the wind and the trees and the earth, but the human mind was beyond his control. All he could do was resist through keen focus, much like he did whenever he was eager to silence Joshua's nagging voice.

Demetry closed his eyes and envisioned the void. His mind became a blank slate, a speck of black, floating in a sea of nothingness. The pressure in his skull faded. The competing voices became silent. Demetry opened his eyes. Cendrik was glaring at him, his lips twitching with frustration.

"Stay out of my head," snarled Demetry. He swung his arms in the air, forcing Cendrik back.

"We all serve someone," said Cendrik. "That is

the world we live in. I am not unkind. I will give you this one last chance." Cendrik reached out his hand, beckoning Demetry to take it. "In truth, it is more than you deserve."

"Take his hand and you will become a slave," whispered Joshua. *"Follow my voice and you will be free."*

Tears sprung from Demetry's eyes unbidden, his sorrow, regret, and rage all bubbling to the surface at once. "Curse you, Cendrik," said Demetry, gasping for breath between words. "You believe that you are the hero in this tale, the righteous man on a righteous quest. But that makes me the villain, doesn't it?"

"Am I wrong?" said Cendrik, withdrawing his offered hand.

"No," said Demetry, admitting what he had always known in his heart. He was the one who raised Joshua from the dead. He was the one who left Shep to die in the woods. He was the one who murdered Clyde, and Sighelm, and so many others within Brothlo. He was the killer. He was the monster. He was the necromancer.

The air took on a dire chill. Gooseflesh shrouded Demetry's frame. His breath blossomed from his mouth in a cloud of icy vapor. The Sundered Soul responded to his call, and throughout the forest stones began to rattle from the ground and slowly take flight. The tree limbs overhead twisted and snapped. Pine needles and dirt twirled in the air, carried upward by countless cyclonic updrafts. And in amongst it all Demetry swore he saw inky black tentacles manipulating the world to match his every whim.

Cendrik raised his hands and backed away, motioning for calm. "Demetry, think about what you are doing."

Demetry's upper lip raised into a snarl. "I have made up my mind," announced Demetry, his voice edged with certainty. "I will live my life free, or I will die in the effort. I will kill any man who tries to stop me. Unfortunately, that begins with you, Cendrik." The floating rocks went shooting toward Cendrik all at once.

"*Mituw wu cet itus*," spoke a voice that cracked like thunder.

The stump of a long dead tree tore from the ground and planted itself in front of Cendrik's cowering body, forming an impenetrable wall. Demetry's hailstorm of rocks chipped away at the trunk like a woodman's axe, ricocheting this way and that. Not a single rock managed to break through and hit its intended target.

One of the battlemages emerged from the forest

and took up a defensive stance beside the warden. He was elderly, gray-bearded with a bald pate and a face sagging with wrinkles. He strode forward with a walking staff in hand. Demetry had to stifle a laugh — the man would have looked right at home giving a lecture at Taper. It was hard to believe he was a trained killer.

The second battlemage materialized to Demetry's left. This man was younger than the first, middle-aged with dark hair and a dark complexion — a Donastian by the look of him. He carried a curved scimitar in his grasp which he used to slash at the air.

Both men wore steel breastplates, the metal engraved with arcane script. Even from a distance Demetry could tell the purpose of the script — they were enchantments meant to protect the wearer from magic. They would make Demetry's elemental attacks less effective, and would all but eliminate Demetry's ability to directly manipulate the bodies of the two men. Demetry cursed under his breath. He would have to use external forces to defeat these men - flying branches, blunt rocks, honed steel.

"Always be the first to strike," advised Joshua.

For once Demetry listened to the whelp's advice. Using his powers, he yanked a spear from the hands of a startled soldier and sent it hurtling toward the Donastian's face. A trained killer, the Donastian was not one to be caught unprepared. He muttered a quick spell and the spear veered right, embedding itself in a tree.

Graybeard clapped his hands together and the tree nearest Demetry split in half. Its upper boughs came collapsing on top of Demetry. If Demetry relied on the New Magic he wouldn't have had time to respond, but the Old Magic worked as quickly as he could think, and the sudden threat to his life drew his mind into sharp focus. Particle by particle he pulled the tree apart. The tree seemed to age a thousand years in an instant, its branches turning to sawdust, its trunk splintering into weightless splinters. What remained of the tree collapsed on top of Demetry with no more force than a rain of feathers.

He brushed the debris from his shoulder, smirking at his own cunning. The two battlemages eyed Demetry with newfound respect. They had underestimated his powers. In truth, so had Demetry. But not again.

Branches tore from tree trunks and went hurtling toward the two battlemages. Graybeard knocked them aside with his staff, while the Donastian turned them to kindling with his scimitar. The two battlemages countered. Their chants rang through the air like the primal war cries of some ancient tribe, their spells coming fast and furious. Demetry scarcely had time to comprehend the nature of one spell before the next one was summoned.

"*Muja dar fapato...*"

Demetry leapt aside and a ball of fire smote the ground were he had been standing a moment earlier.

"*Wefa seftu mati...*"

Demetry slipped and fell as the rocks beneath his feet took flight.

"*Betru. Betru. Betru.*"

The Donastian's scimitar sliced through the air with enough force to chop down a tree. Demetry would have been cleaved in half had he not dodged aside at the last second. The tip of the blade nicked his shoulder, and he felt the all too familiar warmth of blood running down the length of his arm.

Needing a moment to regain his composure, Demetry summoned a gust of wind, stirring up a blinding cloud of dirt and pine needles. His foes were momentarily blinded. He used the brief respite to rethink his strategy. Every spell his opponents cast required spoken words. It forecasted their intent, granting Demetry a split-second warning of what was coming next. But the speed with which they attacked left Demetry struggling to keep up, let alone strike back.

"*Majrl rit sae.*"

A flash of white hot lightning pierced the debris cloud, narrowly missing Demetry's head. It struck a tree instead, causing all of the bark to pop free from the trunk with a sizzling hiss. A second bolt came flying in right behind the first, then a third, and a fourth, and a fifth. Graybeard was blindly lashing out. Demetry kept feeding wind into the tumult, hoping that the swirling wall of debris would obscure his true position.

The Donastian leapt into the fray, his scimitar pinwheeling as he tried to cut Demetry down. He interchanged his sword swings with incendiary spells. It took all of Demetry's strength to stay one step ahead of the attacks. The forest became engulfed in flames as stray pyromantic blasts landed amongst dry timber and dead pine needles. The heat of leaping flames raged all about him. Demetry's hair began to singe and curl in on itself. His eyebrows melted away. His clothing began to smoke and fray.

There was a purpose to the Donastian's seemingly haphazard attacks — he was forcing Demetry's back to Graybeard.

"Use their strategy against them."

Demetry doubled over and grabbed at his chest, feigning exhaustion. The Donastian took the bait. He lashed out with a ball of leaping flames. Demetry avoided the worst of the blast by dropping to the ground. He channeled the Sundered Soul, and all at once the wind changed course, carrying with it the swirling maelstrom of pine-needles and debris. The gust fed into the fireball, redirecting the blast and intensifying the heat of the flames a hundredfold.

Graybeard simply stood there with a stunned expression on his face as the fireball grew larger and larger. It swallowed his body whole. When the flames finally abated, Demetry was not surprised to find Graybeard still standing on his feet. Graybeard's enchanted armor had served its purpose and absorbed the majority of the blast, which was precisely what Demetry hoped would happen. Steel was terribly efficient at conducting heat, and the breastplate was glowing like the face of a blast furnace.

Graybeard hollered in agony as he frantically fumbled with the straps holding the breastplate in place. The glowing breastplate peeled away from his chest, taking with it a seared layer of flesh. Graybeard stared with horror at his injury, unaware of how irrelevant the wound actually was. He was dead the moment he took off his armor, he just didn't know it yet.

Demetry focused on the blood coursing through Graybeard's veins, exciting the individual particles until they began to boil. Graybeard's eyes bugged as the pain began to register. Steam poured from his mouth and nostrils. His skin became covered with hideous blisters and bubbles. He collapsed to the ground and clawed at his face, his fingers coming away with great sloughs of flesh.

The Donastian's mouth hung open as he watched the carnage unfold. He was dumbfounded, and why wouldn't he be? There were no New Magic spells capable of manipulating the fluids coursing through a man's veins. Graybeard's demise was a product of the Old Magic. His demise was the product of a truly twisted mind.

"How?" asked the Donastian as his comrade gave a final shudder and succumbed to his wounds.

"The Old Magic," answered Demetry.

The Donastian nodded, perhaps understanding then that his fate was already sealed.

The ground beneath the Donastian's feet liquefied and turned into quicksand. Before knew what was happening the earth had swallowed him up to his knees. He tried to pull his legs free only to fall over and sink to his waist, and then his chest, and finally his neck. The Donastian tried to chant a spell that might save his life, but Demetry didn't allow a word to leave his mouth. A river of gravel and dirt poured down the Donastian's throat, choking off the words.

"*Our first victory,*" whispered Joshua.

Demetry nodded his head in agreement.

The forest was now engulfed in flames, a hellscape of burning trees and collapsing limbs. Black smoke shrouded all, turning everyone into indistinct and faceless shapes. Some of Cendrik's men were already running. More appeared eager to join in the retreat. Only a few stood their ground.

Demetry yelled into the madness, his eyes searching for the warden. "Did your seer's mind tell you this was how it was going to end, Cendrik?" He could hardly hear his own voice over the crackling din of the raging fire.

"This is not an ending," answered Cendrik.

Demetry spun in place, his eyes searching the smoke shrouded figures who stood in a ring around him. He was unable to discern which man was the warden.

"Nor is this a beginning," continued Cendrik. "This is just a step in the middle of your journey. You should be thanking me. I could have kept you locked away in a black cell. Instead, I introduced you to Jeremiah. I helped make you into a god."

Demetry beckoned with his hand. "Come then, Cendrik, reap what you have sown. Come and meet your god." Demetry's eyes narrowed on a lone figure, certain it was the warden.

Cendrik's scornful laugh echoed in Demetry's head. "My king is my god, Demetry. Just as he is yours."

Demetry had the wrong man — Cendrik's voice had come from the right. He spun in that direction only to discover a wall of burning trees.

"I have my own tricks, too."

Cendrik's voice was in his head, realized Demetry, much too late. Which meant...

Something closed around Demetry's neck, locking tight with a metallic click. The wave of nausea was immediate. Demetry crumpled to his knees, all his strength vanishing at once. Cendrik had drawn Demetry's attention in one direction and crept up behind him from the other.

"Foresight is nearly as powerful as the Old Magic," said Cendrik, whispering directly into Demetry's ear. A lopsided and triumphant grin was plastered on his face. "You go left and I go right. You try to use magic, and I cut off the power at its source."

Demetry pawed at the gelding collar, his fingers fumbling at the clasp. Cendrik swatted Demetry's hand aside like a schoolmaster correcting an errant student. He stepped on Demetry's back, forcing him down on all fours.

The forest's upper canopy was now fully engulfed in fire. Cinders and ash rained down from above causing the underbrush to erupt in flames. The inferno crept closer by the second.

"Do you want to know why I chose you, Demetry?" Cendrik growled through clenched teeth. "Do you want to know how I knew you were capable of mastering the Old Magic?"

"Let me guess — you read my mind."

Cendrik ground his heel into Demetry's spine, causing Demetry to cry out in pain. "Jeremiah was right, I am a terrible seer. But there is one premonition I always get right. Death. I've seen you die, Demetry, and when you do, you will be second to the gods in power."

An involuntary laugh escaped Demetry's throat, making him sound like a madman. "Ha! Then that means you're not going to kill me. At least not today."

"No," agreed Cendrik. "But that does not mean I can't put you through unimaginable pain in the interim." Cendrik picked up a burning stick and thrust it toward Demetry's face. "I'll start with the left eye. The Orb — where is it?"

Demetry could feel the heat of the flame wicking away the moisture in his eye. The point of the flaming stick crept closer and closer. "Luthuania!" blurted Demetry, hoping to buy time. "The elves have it! Jeremiah gave it to the elves!"

Cendrik didn't reply — his attention was drawn elsewhere.

The sound of clashing steel sounded to the east. Cendrik squinted toward the noise, his eyelids twitching. The triumphant grin faded from his face. His hand shifted to the pommel of his dagger. "Men, check the perimeter!" His order went unheeded — his voice was lost over the crackling roar of the flames.

Demetry motioned toward the heavens as the fire raged all around them, a maelstrom of smoke and cinders and flaming debris. "Only foolish men travel into the realm of the elves unbidden!"

More clashes of steel. The wretched cry of a dying man pierced the air.

"Stay low and be quiet," hissed Cendrik. "We're not alone." His eyes were as wide as saucers. He drew his dagger, pointing it toward the shadowed figures that were hemming them in. "I've seen this before. I've..." The words died in his throat, replaced by a wet gargle. Demetry was shocked to discover a feathered shaft had grown out of Cendrik's neck. Cendrik grasped at the arrow and stumbled backward, tripping over a rock and falling atop a bed of burning debris.

Demetry gasped in dismay as more arrows fell amongst Cendrik's men, some of the deadly projectiles taking light as they crashed through the burning canopy. And with the arrows came cloaked figures. They came pouring down the hillside, as nimble and quick as wildcats. They leapt through the flames, swords flashing with orange light.

Elves, was Demetry's first thought. The cloaked figures stampeded through the burning forest, hacking and slashing at anything that moved. Demetry unlatched the gelding collar from around his neck and tried to crawl away. The collar had served its purpose, his magic was gone. He would be helpless to defend himself, so he stayed low, praying that he might go unnoticed.

The massacre continued. Steel chimed. Men cried and died all around him. The remnants of Cendrik's hunting party were now in full retreat. The cloaked figures did not let them go far. Bow strings twanged and the fleeing men were struck dead by long-feathered shafts. Few if any managed to escape — the slaughter was absolute.

Demetry cursed himself for coming this way. No one ventured into the forbidden realm of the elves without paying a bloody price.

CHAPTER
XII

THE MONSTER AND THE NECROMANCER

Demetry cowered behind a downed tree, silently praying that he would go unseen. The sound of clashing steel became intermittent, then stopped altogether. The grunts and groans of dying men faded. The crackle of burning trees was overwhelming to the ears. Demetry could feel the first inkling of magic returning to his body. Just a little bit longer and he would be able to defend himself.

Heavy footsteps sounded just beyond the downed tree. The unseen figure sniffed at the air, like a hound on a scent. A new tremor of fear worked through Demetry's body.

"There is no need to hide, young magic," The speaker's voice lacked the urbane and sing-songy inflection of the elven accent. Instead, the voice was gruff, almost harsh on the ears. Whoever the speaker was, he was clearly unaccustomed to conversing in the common tongue.

Demetry peered over the downed tree, unsure of what to expect. A cloaked figure was standing on the far side. He motioned for Demetry to rise. Seeing no other option, Demetry gathered his feet and turned to face this new foe.

"Stay back," said Demetry, balling his fists at his side. "I'm a magic. If you give me a reason to kill you, I will not hesitate."

The cloaked figure gave a hissing laugh, his face still concealed within the shadows of his hood. He gestured to the dead and dying men that lay all around them. "I have given you ample reason to kill me, yet you hesitate. Perhaps you do nothing because you currently lack the ability." He held up the gelding collar, pinching it between a pair of clawed fingers.

A cold shiver ran through Demetry's body. This creature was no elf.

The figure shouldered off his cloak, revealing a monstrous body. Cold reptilian eyes. Toes and fingers studded by claws. Skin the color of ash. A face that tapered to a pointed beak. A pair of featherless wings sprouted from the creature's shoulders, each headed by a bony talon. Demetry had never seen such a creature before, yet he knew exactly what he was facing. A dark child. A creature of the Wyrm. A dragoon.

Demetry stifled a gasp. This seemed to please the dragoon. His reptilian face curled into what could best be described as a grin. "I am Tyronious, chieftain of the Vierno Clan," said the dragoon, placing his hand over his heart. "I come as a friend." As if to prove that point, he tossed the gelding collar into the flames. The light in the Sundering Stone extinguished when it met the heat of the fire. Tyronious motioned to his men with his clawed hand. "We have been searching for you ever since we received word of your escape."

Many of the other dragoons had also cast aside their cloaks. Victory was theirs. They no longer had any reason to conceal their true identities. The dragoons walked amongst the dead, cutting ribbons of cloth from the clothes of their victims. This seemed to be a sign of merit amongst the dragoons. They tied the ribbons around their biceps and wing blades. Some wore only a few, others had dozens. Tyronious's trophies were too numerous to count. He possessed ribbons of every imaginable fabric and hue. They were knotted together, forming a chain of fabric that hung from his back like a cape.

Demetry eyed the savage creature with distrust.

"Why were you searching for me?"

"Not you, to be honest, but your master. Where is General Jeremiah?"

Hearing Jeremiah's name was like a punch to the gut, but Demetry kept himself from showing the slightest hint of emotion. Dragoons were savages and killers — or so Demetry was taught in school. They had no respect for sorrow or remorse. A show of weakness now might get Demetry killed.

"An archer with a lucky shot was able to accomplish what a legion of the king's best men could not," said Demetry. "Jeremiah is dead. He was killed in our flight from Coljack." Demetry could only pray that the truth didn't forfeit his value to the dragoons, at least not until his power returned in full.

If Tyronious was disheartened by the news, his reptilian face did not reveal it. "Jeremiah's death is... unfortunate," he said, after a moment of silence. "We have traveled through the barren wastes of Eremor and the hostile realms of our enemies only to discover our efforts have been in vain. A pity."

"What did you want from him?"

"Death. Ruin. Conquest." Tyronious smirked. "The dark children were laid low by the men of Caper. My people slaughtered, the survivors scattered. But time has been kind to us. We have multiplied. The trials of the northern wastes have made us strong. Legions are gathering. War is coming. Jeremiah was to be our champion."

"You intend to wage war on King Johan?" Demetry shook his head. "Death awaits whomever chooses that path."

"Do I look afraid of death?" Tyronious motioned to the dragoons who were still shuffling amongst the bodies of the slain with wet blades. "We are death's servant. We are children of the Wyrm. The immortal gods created us with a splinter of their essence. Our bodies may expire, but our souls are boundless, immortal, just as the gods we once served."

The gods Tyronious's people once served were most definitely dead, blasted to ash in the War of Sundering. Demetry decided it was best not to correct the dark child on the matter. "If you are so fearless, why do you need Jeremiah?"

Tyronious clacked his reptilian beak. "General Jeremiah was the Wyrm's chosen son. His mastery of the Old Magic was without compare. Our forefathers served under General Jeremiah's command. He brought us victory and glory beyond imagine. Currently, the dragoon clans are fractured. There are those who think I will lead our people to ruin. But if I were to return north with the general at my side, no one would dare speak out against my plan." He grinned. "Jeremiah's death is a setback, but Fate has afforded me great gifts. I have been denied the master, but given the protege."

"Me?"

"Are you going to feign ignorance? The voiceless power of the Old Magic runs strong in you. What if I told you I could increase your strength a hundredfold? That I could grant you mastery of vast legions? That empires would tremble at the mention of your name and that kings would quail in your presence?"

"I would say you weave an intoxicating tale full of lies."

"The most manipulative lies are the ones that stoke a man's thirst." Tyronious edged closer, like a serpent cornering its prey. "The Orb of Azure has an allure like few other artifacts. He who holds it would be akin to the gods."

Demetry's eyes narrowed. Cendrik had said Demetry would eventually attain power that was second only to the gods. Was the Orb the means by which he would achieve such strength? "You know where the Orb is hidden?"

The corner of Tyronious's mouth curled with delight. "My eyes are everywhere. My ears hear all. I see the conspiring king and the lurking assassin. I hear the woeful cries of slaves and the unrequited prayers of the desperate. Even you, Demetry, were not beyond my omniscience. Your suffering within Coljack did not go unseen. What they did to you. What they made you do..." He motioned to the bodies of Cendrik and the two battlemages. "Thus far your rage has been misdirected, your revenge taken out on mere stooges of the crown. I encourage you to set your sights higher. King Johan is as mortal as any man, and you, Demetry, are only one step short of godhood."

Demetry could feel his power returning. He was no longer defenseless. If he so desired, he could kill every last dragoon where they stood. He could freeze their hearts in their chests, or force them to fall on their own blades.

"But why kill what you can force to serve," whispered Joshua. Demetry couldn't agree more.

"You seek a champion, Tyronious. But who would that champion serve? You? Your people?" Demetry shook his head. "I will not serve another man in my life. If I am to accompany you north, I go as Jeremiah's heir, inheritor of his rank and esteem."

Tyronious mulled over the offer for a moment, chewing on his tongue. "There will be those amongst my people who will have doubts."

"Then I will convince them," replied Demetry.

"They will want proof of your power, your strength."

"I am eager to demonstrate my skill." A dire chill swept over the forest, and one by one the fires guttered into nothingness. A collective gasp rose amongst Tyronious's band of warriors as they looked about themselves in wonder.

"People may have to die," said Tyronious.

"I will not hesitate to do what must be done."

Tyronious nodded his head and offered Demetry his hand to seal the compact.

"The master does not shake the hand of his slave."

Joshua's advice was beginning to sound more and more sensible.

Demetry ignored Tyronious's outstretched hand and walked past the dragoon. He wove his way amongst the downed limbs, smoldering debris, and stiff bodies. He walked within feet of Cendrik's corpse without giving it more than a passing glance. The warden had lived an unfortunate existence, wasting his life in the service of another man. Demetry would not make the same mistake. From this point forward he would think only of his own well-being.

"Of our well-being," added Joshua.

Demetry nodded in agreement.

He strode by the ravaged bodies of the two battlemages the king had sent to kill him. There was a lesson here as well. The battlemages had died because they were not as strong as the opponent they faced. Demetry would not stop training until he was the most powerful magic alive. Cendrik had foreseen this future, but only Demetry could make it a reality.

Finally, he approached the clearing where the dragoon warriors were gathering. The hulking figures were festooned with bloody ribbons they had collected from their victims. They were a terrifying sight. Demetry had to fight off the instinct to quail beneath their ferocious gaze. He had lived his entire life staring down at his own feet, showing a meek face and a docile temper to anyone who presented themselves as a threat. No more. *Let them fear me instead.* He held his head high, clenching his jaw and staring down any dragoon that would meet his eye.

Tyronious chased after Demetry, his shoulders sagging a little, his face seeming less fierce, less proud, subservient even. "Come, let me introduce you to my people. You are Jeremiah's successor, and are thus worthy of a grand title. What shall my people call you — lord, master, warlock?"

Warden Cendrik was right, Demetry was reborn, just not in the fashion the seer had intended. Demetry swore allegiance to no one. Served no one. Prayed to no one. He was his own man. His destiny was his, and only his to control. Demetry shrugged off the weight of his old life and embraced the uncertain future that lay ahead.

He walked past the dragoons, forcing Tyronious and his warriors to follow in his wake. "A man's title only has value if it can provoke a worthwhile reaction from his friends and foes," said Demetry, his voice mimicking the fine intonation that Jeremiah so often used while giving a lecture. "For now, I will need to be feared. Our foes must dread my wrath, so that compliance will seem a better option than resistance."

Demetry turned to face his entourage of eagerly awaiting dragoons. "Your people shall call me the Necromancer," announced Demetry. The god-fearing men of this world deemed necromancy an unforgivable sin. He would wear it as a badge.

"A suitable title," said Tyronious, nodding with satisfaction. "It will set fear in the hearts of your foes."

"*Indeed it will*," added Joshua. "*But such a title must be temporary. One day, when the Orb of Azure is in your possession, you will need a more friendly title. King, perhaps.*

Or maybe emperor."

"How about god?" whispered Demetry in reply. For once the voices in his head did not sound any objection. Instead, they gave him a hearty round of applause.

AFTERWORD

Thank you for reading *A Wizard's Dark Dominion*. The rest of the series is available now in both print and ebook formats, while other books in the world of Laveria are currently in the works. For more information on my upcoming novels, visit www.leehhaywood.com. There you can sign up for my newsletter to receive notifications about future sales events, send me an email, or connect with me on Facebook and Twitter. I would love to hear from you.

Also, if you enjoyed the book, please consider telling a friend or providing a review on Amazon and Goodreads. Reviews are the lifeblood of indie publishing, and your feedback can help make or break a book. Your input is greatly appreciated.

Thank you for your support!

EAGER TO KNOW WHAT HAPPENS NEXT?

PLEASE ENJOY THIS PREVIEW OF

THE GUARDIAN
THE GODS AND KINGS CHRONICLES BOOK 1

AVAILABLE NOW IN PRINT AND EBOOK FORMATS.

CHAPTER

I

MANHERM

The wall had failed.

The acrid smell of rot wafted from the field beyond, intermingling with the scent of sweat and iron. Below, a horse screamed, its body broken upon a spear. Karlan didn't notice. He sat upright, slouched against the cold stone walls of the battlement, his head shifted skyward, taking in the dawning light with voided eyes. A poison arrow protruded from his forearm. An ignoble death, thought Bently as he eyed the general's body warily.

"He's gone. Throw him over with the others," said Disias.

A collapsed siege engine lay burning beyond the wall, belching a column of black smoke into the air. They had been feeding it all night; ladders, refuse, fresh oil, and always more bodies. A few of the men still writhed and twisted in the inferno, desperate to crawl nowhere in particular, yet unable to free themselves from the entangled debris. Half of his division lay somewhere within the pyre.

"It's not decent," said Bently, rejecting the idea. He ran his hand through his short cropped hair, feeling the knots of scar tissue on his head.

"Decency has no part in it. A plague is a plague. Throw him over." Disias nervously rubbed his hands together, warding off a chill that wasn't there.

"Lord Disias is right, sir," said Eldin, nodding to himself. He sat perched upon the battlement a few feet from the dead body, his feet dangling over the edge. His hands trembled as he absentmindedly whetted the same blade again and again. "Being highborn has nothing to do with it."

Bently turned away from the conscript, ignoring his opinion. "We wait. It might be different this time," Bently muttered almost to himself. He knew it wouldn't. He bent over and collected the medallion pinned to Karlan's chest, taking care to swat aside a fly that crawled across the dead man's lips.

Bently rubbed his finger over the insignia, a red bear set beside a white tower. Karlan's family would cherish the keepsake. Of course, it was a civilized gesture, made in deference to a world that no longer existed. The truth was, Karlan's family was somewhere in Manherm, and Manherm was falling to pieces. They would never get the memento. They would never hear that Bently had done their father honor by not throwing him into the fire like a commoner. *Guardsmen stick together in life and death.* He placed the medallion in his pocket.

Disias snarled. "That doesn't make you the commander."

"No, it certainly does not," replied Bently coolly. Bently's hand shifted to his sword, his palm conforming to the familiar ivory grip. A hush fell over the gathering of soldiers. Disias's fingers twitched near his hilt. Bently scowled. *Steel is the only thing men are bound to respect in times like these.*

An acquiescent smile creased Disias's face and he skirted out of reach, rapping his knuckle against the rondel of his sword. He bowed mockingly. "I'm going to Weaver's Hall, captain. Best to make peace with the gods while one can. Time is short." He bounded down the rampart steps before Bently could react, becoming lost in the passing confluence of people.

The streets below were packed to a near standstill. A man vainly attempted to shove through the crowd with a squealing sow under each arm. A women lamented for her missing child who had fallen underfoot. A horse panicked as it was blindly pushed along with the flow of traffic. Its headstall was yanked over its eyes, and a dead knight was seated backward upon its saddle, swaying lithely. Yanish brothers, garbed in yellow robes and conical caps, filtered amongst the masses in a parade of zealotry. Dirge bells chimed, flutes whistled, and all the while there was the ever-present smack of leather striking bare skin. Many of the atoning brothers had stripped to their loincloths and were flagellating themselves with barbed thongs for their transgressions. Bewildered orphans trailed in their wake like obedient ducklings, their bald heads raw and inflamed from a fresh shave. They were off to receive their final absolution, blissfully unaware of what that would portend. All were heading in the wrong direction, but no sensible words could turn this tide. Bently let the issue rest. The world was ending.

Smoke plumed to the east, casting a shadow over the city. The sphere of the sun dimmed. The eastern portcullis was raised, the wooden gate broken asunder. Black figures streamed through the opening uncontested. The white walls of Stone Keep shimmered in dancing flames, reflecting off the chopped waters of the Jasmine. The river meandered along the city's south face, carrying in it the bobbing jetsam of desperate people. Skiffs and flatboats jammed the quay, and deckhands were throwing everything overboard to create space for the press of refugees. Some of the braver sailors cycled to and fro across the river, ferrying people to safety, while others abandoned their ships on the far shore and ran for their lives.

The press on the dock intensified. Bodies began to plummet into the churning water, a cascade of flailing arms and legs. Black shapes were suddenly teeming in amongst the people, biting and gouging. A terrible wail rose from the crowd, coalescing into a constant hum like the thrumming buzz of a hornet's nest. Humanity always toed a delicate line, and now the last modicum of civility vanished. People clambered over each other, frantic to escape.

Most of the men atop the wall looked on, stupefied. Their stolid faces showed no semblance of comprehension. "Do we go to their aid?" said Duffry, an obtuse man who hadn't the sense to know there was nothing they could do.

"No use...no use at all," stuttered Eldin. He had seen too much for one lifetime, and viewed the chaos with a degree of aloofness. "The battle has moved on, captain. No use to stay here either. No use to stay anywhere, in truth." He set his hands on a ladder left from the enemy's failed assault. The man's crazed eyes shifted nervously from the field to Bently and back again, waiting to see if Bently would stop him. All enmity passed from Bently's heart. These men were conscripts; they had sworn no oaths of loyalty. Bently gestured for Eldin to leave, consenting to the man's cowardice. Without further hesitation, Eldin squeezed his legs through the crenelation and scampered down the ladder to the ground. Another followed, then another, until the whole battlement was emptied save Bently and Karlan.

Bently watched the men zigzag as they dashed amongst the bodies in the killing field, sending carrion birds into a pluming contrail. The birds cawed and screeched, their bodies bloated from the feast. The men gave the Wraith King a wide berth.

Set in the middle of the field hung the body of King Johan, placed there so the whole city could bear witness to his turn. His brow was still twisted in a grimace. His purple cape fluttered in the wind, tugging fruitlessly against the gold clasp that held it fastened to galled flesh. His ruby-studded crown rested askew atop his head, offset by the spear that protruded from his shoulder. He was spitted atop the hill like a macabre scarecrow. The white bone of his chest stood in stark relief against a cavity of red. About his dangling feet lie the vanquished banners of his house, crushed into the mire.

There lies my loyalty, Bently thought. *There lies the death of one world.*

Johan's head lifted, casting his visionless gaze over the killing field. Finally, the pallid orbs of his eyes settled upon Bently. His jaw shifted and the sinew of his neck bulged. Slowly his cankered lips parted, his blue tongue rising and falling in a slow purposeful drawl, mouthing the same pattern Bently had seen countless times now. The words were lost on the wind. A cold shiver ran down Bently's spine.

"When the dead live, may the gods have mercy." Bently looked away from the unsettling apparition.

On the horizon, the tear-shaped outline of a willow was barely visible. He imagined two figures stood beneath it awaiting favorable news. By now they had doubtlessly seen the pall of smoke that belied any hope. He reached toward the tree contritely. He should have sent them to the Nexus. Now it was too late.

Bently stroked the wood of the ladder. Hard pine, soaked in water to ward off flame. It would be simple; one leg over the divide, and then the next. He would have to outrun the scavengers, but they were preoccupied. A thousand men lay dying on the field, pleading for help. This seemed to only enliven the sanguinary lust of the foragers. Figures with serpentine faces roamed the butchered bodies like vultures, stripping away swatches of cloth from the wounded. One by one the murmuring voices were extinguished. The dragoons emerged swaddled in the cloth of their victims.

In the distance a bell tolled fervently, alerting the townspeople of fire. He wondered what tractable fool manned the bell tower, extolling a needless warning to a doomed city. The world was ending, and the bellman thought it wise to welcome it. Bently wished he possessed such blind loyalty, but his loyalty lie far afield, beneath the boughs of that tree.

He ignominiously set one foot on the ladder rung.

There was a rustle beside him. Karlan's tongue was clacking against the roof of his mouth and his teeth began to gnash. Pale fingers involuntarily dug into the hard stone slabs of the rampart, ceaselessly delving into the unrelenting surface until his fingernails tore loose. With a lurch Karlan rose to his feet, as if the necromancer had come and whispered an incantation directly in his ear, bidding him to rise.

Death and rebirth, thought Bently. He sighed

despondently and alighted the ladder. Girding himself, he raised his greatsword above his head. He wondered if there was anything left of Karlan behind those voided eyes. He blinked away the disquieting thought and split Karlan from neck to armpit with one heavy swipe.

The two halves of Karlan's body fell from the battlements, almost striking a startled boy who was sprinting up the rampart stairs.

The boy looked at the body in disgust, clearly noting the epaulettes that beset each of Karlan's separated shoulders. "Where are your men, captain?" said the boy to Bently.

Bently looked at him queerly. A stunted youth, barely old enough to swear the oath of brotherhood. A lie would suffice to get the courier to go away.

"Dead on the field."

"General Waymire has ordered all men to gather at the Waterways."

"Lady Manherm?"

"We are rallying to her banner."

"A final push for the lordess?" mulled Bently. Waymire somehow defrayed the lives of a hundred thousand people against that of Evelyn Manherm, willfully surrendering the city to aid her escape. Bently was certain her life did not measure equally to the two lives he would be leaving behind if he followed Waymire's command. He looked to the willow wistfully, but it was gone, hidden behind a shifting haze.

This is how the world ends, realized Bently. Not the earth, for it was timeless and without limit. But his world. The world of smiling faces and careless laughter, of warm embraces and days worth living. *This is how men die without dying.*

He turned away from the willow, wiping all sign of dourness from his face, and took on the stern countenance of a captain. "My sword is ever hers to command."

He pushed the ladder away from the wall, sending it clattering into the conflagration. He followed the courier, going in the opposite direction that his heart commanded.

He did not see the willow beset by a sea of flame.

He did not see his world come to an end, yet he felt it all the same.

THE SAGA CONTINUES IN

THE GUARDIAN
THE GODS AND KINGS CHRONICLES BOOK 1

BOOKS IN THE SERIES

THE ORDER - A STANDALONE PREQUEL

A WIZARD'S DARK DOMINION
THE GUARDIAN
THE GUARDIAN STONE

Available in ebook and softbound formats.

Visit **www.leehhaywood.com** for more details.

Made in the USA
Coppell, TX
26 July 2020